SHOOT THE PRESIDENT, ARE YOU MAD?

by

FRANK MCAULIFFE

SHOOT THE PRESIDENT, ARE YOU MAD?

by

FRANK MCAULIFFE

THE OUTFIT

SHOOT THE PRESIDENT, ARE YOU MAD?

The Outfit
www.outfitcrime.com

ISBN: 978-1-60701-151-4

BEFORE Clifford Waxout died escaping my arms, he screeched, "...bastard...you lousy *bastard...*" It was a farewell fraught with genealogical inaccuracy, but one of enviable vigor, under the circumstances. (The brisk descent from the picturesque cliff; the sudden, definitive embrace of the rocks....)

I shrouded his remains carefully in masonry and lowered them to the floor of the gentle Pacific. I interred all but the name, Clifford Waxout. Prior to our encounter, his name was known to perhaps 2,000 souls. Not an insignificant multitude, to be sure. But consider: before I released my grip on Clifford, his name, why, it did ring throughout the land.

That same afternoon I drove Clifford's Buick to his home in Portland, Oregon and parked the vehicle on his blacktopped driveway.

His wife Nell, a woman of 42 who celebrated each year with another fold of ripe flesh, popped through the front door. She advanced on me and the Buick, stuffing her toy-balloon fingers into tight white gloves.

"My God, Cliff," she pouted, "I thought you'd never get home. My car has a flat tire and I'm late for Winnie's Best Seller Party."

There was just a chance it was a *Best Cellar Party.* I never found out. Ah, Winnie, you sly vixen, what evil brew do you and your ladies ferment in your gloomy, cob-webbed basement?

Nell brushed past me; past the painted and be-wigged man she took to be her husband, and grunted her way onto the front seat of the Buick. Obviously I had wasted some of the effort spent in aging and repositioning my features to achieve a surface resemblance to Clifford Waxout.

The engine was ignited and my Nell powered the vehicle backwards out of the driveway until she was lined up like a thoroughbred in the starting gate at the STOP sign at the next corner. As the Buick roared off, one pudgy little white hand wiggled over Nell's head. Her last adieu to her husband, though she knew it not. Rather a rude one, I couldn't help but feel.

Clifford, Clifford, you are now delivered from such incivility. Rest in peace, my son.

I entered the Waxout home. The interior was rather familiar to me. I had visited the house on three occasions:

Tuesday: The City Property Assessor presented his credentials. "...Just a general look-see, Mrs. Waxout. New alignment of the property tax structure, ya know? Can I get me a look at your backyard? Any new bird baths?..."

Thursday: The fuel oil company Tank Inspector chanced by for a look-see at the heater in the basement. "...Ya got a leaky H-valve. Nothing to worry about. Everybody in this end-a the city got it. Must be something that's going around..."

Friday: The telephone company Troubleshooter stopped off. "... Just a look-see at the extensions in the upstairs bedrooms, Ma'm. Lot of people getting noise on the lines. Dots and dashes. Could be those little birds walking on the wires. Then maybe it's Commie spies...."

It was a fairly decent looking home. One of the advantages of living in America (Come, come, old man, there *are* some.) is they do tend to hammer together rather acceptable enclosures for the housing of their citizens. Actually one gets the impression the specifications governing construction practices reflect more a concern for the income generating elements of the home: telephones, furnaces, hot water pipes, electrical outlets and the like. The inhabitants merely fall heir to the residual comforts.

From Clifford Waxout's wardrobe (the man had the taste of a guildsman, possibly a cobbler) I selected three suits, a topcoat, and the miscellaneous appointments to supplement them. The garments would eventually be delivered to some east coast pawn broker, some gentleman whose trade had immunized him to indignity. The junkman might remember the sale when the police inquired and provide my description. Should he not, it would not matter. There would be a sufficient number of others to provide eye witness accounts. With Clifford's rags locked in a durable suitcase retrieved from the basement, I awaited the taxi that would supply the initial mileage in my departure from the city of Portland, Oregon. Not an unattractive metropolis, although a bit on the Nordic side, for my taste.

Prior to the arrival of the taxi, I penned the following note to dear Nell and left it by the telephone:

Nell.
Going to Baltimore to straighten out the Wall-Pool contract. Call Hoffman and tell him. I'll call you Tuesday night when the train gets in. Be gone a couple of weeks. You can use the Buick but get the God damn flat on the Plymouth fixed.
Cliff

Terse, bubbling with ice pick sentimentality, so like Clifford. The "Hoffman" mentioned in the note was Fred Hoffman, Superintendent of Production at Waxout Industries. He would run the factory while the boss was away. I would call Fred on Tuesday also, to report that the situation at Wall-Pool was more chaotic than anticipated and would require my presence in Baltimore for several weeks.

Waxout Industries was a small Portland firm that manufactured compact industrial air condition units. The two units installed at the Wall-Pool Laboratory in Baltimore were, to the best of my knowledge, performing as specified in the Waxout Industry's catalog. Should my faithful Superintendent of Production, Fred Hoffman, contact the folk at Wall-Pool looking for me, even the embarrassing knowledge that I had not been seen in Baltimore would precipitate no further inquiry on Fred's part. Clifford Waxout had been the boss of his factory, the boss in the fine old tradition; the ramrod, iron fist, martinet tradition. How sad that we have replaced such entrepreneurs with that "cowardly huddle" of modern business. I refer of course to that shot-gun spray decision-making group vis-a-vis the single-line, well-drilled hole of the long rifleman. That slothful clutch with its murky lines of responsibility; the last refuge of the ass and bumpkin: The Board of Directors.

Fred Hoffman, commendably, would not dare question the boss. Therein one of the considerations that had placed Clifford Waxout on the floor of the Pacific; a tide-swaying bundle stirring slowly in the grip of the ocean; a curio to passing fish; a slim, tasty herb contributing to Man's never ending efforts to manipulate the consistency of the planet's great bodies of water. Speaking of things nautical, there remained one mooring line to cast off before I left. When the taxi materialized, I directed the driver from the Waxout home to an office building in downtown Portland.

On the seventh floor of the building, I made my way past a pebble-glass door on which this letter appeared: *America's Americans—Northwest Division.*

The air of the small outer foyer was stale and there was no one in attendance at the single chipped-veneer desk on which the rings made by coffee cups overlapped in a foolish pattern. On the wall adjacent to the door, hung a framed document titled, *Credo of a Real American.* It read in part: "...He/she shall discard all allegiances; family, friend, religious, when service to his *American Allegiance* requires it..."

Another framed poster identified the players involved in this bush-league patriotism. It was an organization chart of *America's Americans*. Headquarters was located in Washington, D.C. (Where else, old boy?) The remainder of the United States was divided into eight divisions. (In the period covered by this narrative you hold so devotedly, dear reader, the United States numbered a mere 48.

The Americans had yet to respond to the lonely cries of the Alaskan pioneers for respite from the rigors of qualified independence. And, of course, the acquisition of the state of Hawaii was some years off, at least in the minds of the happy-go-lucky Hawaiians.) Clifford Waxout was listed as Director of Northwest. Beneath his name were listed four staff members, most prominent of these being the post of Secretary of Northwest.

The organization chart had no glass in its frame. Evidently it required frequent updating. A number of names had been painted out with some white substance and new names lettered on top of the old.

Fan-spread pamphlets were arranged on a small table in the foyer next to a potted plant. The pamphlets were designed to alert complacent Americans (the "fat, dumb and happy" chaps we hear so much about) to a terror that stalked the land. I recognized one of the booklets as one I had read but two weeks previous. The title was: *They Are Making Enemy Agents of Americans Overseas!*

The booklet contained an editorial plea for Congressional legislation that would designate any absence from continental United States for a period longer than six months as grounds for mandatory loss of citizenship.

The authors of the pamphlet admitted that a probable exception would have to be granted to those involved in military duty in a foreign outpost. But this exception, they insisted, should not exceed a one-year's absence. "...Even our brave American soldiers, if overexposed to the Satanic influence of foreigners, can stray from the guiding principles that have made America this Great Land We Love..." (The demanded legislation, I understand, is still pending in Congress.)

Clifford Waxout had been the Northwest Director of these suspicious malcontents; the engine that pulled the tumbrel. But it was the Secretary of Northwest who pumped into the engine the flammable fuel. Her name was listed on the organization chart, Mrs. Polly Culver. Clifford lent his spare time. Polly Culver was underpaid, over-worked, ten-hour-a-day steel mesh to which the facade of the Northwest Division clung.

If I were to successfully relocate the identity of Clifford Waxout for several weeks, it was necessary to ground some of the voltage in this female generator.

Polly was at her desk in an inner glassed-in office. In the area between the foyer and Polly's office were three desks at which sat three hired hacks. Should the zeal of the coolies stagger or pause, they had but to glance through a glass partition to view the mother lode of dedication. There sat the secretary, nailed, nay, crucified to her desk by ramrod concentration.

I strode through the outer office, smiling to the underlings, and entered the office of my Secretary. During my passage, my eye rambled freely over the one female employee, a maid of twenty or so summers, whose downcast gaze preserved her from knowledge of my hot-eyed grip on her bosom.

Now, Augustus, a test of how well you have manufactured this product you call Clifford Waxout. His secretary knew him. I had been unable to plum the Clifford Waxout/Polly Culver relationship any deeper than an assessment of their successful manipulation of *America's Americans,* Northwest Division. They worked well together. Clifford was mentioned within the organization as the logical choice for the Directorship at National Headquarters when the incumbent retired.

But was this enough for Clifford and Polly; this team grip of the Northwest pressure nozzle through which they sprayed a thoughtful volume of patriotic anarchy out upon the senses of their fellow citizens? How does one measure the warmth, the companionship, generated by rubbing two zealots together shoulder-to-shoulder?

Each had a spouse to consider, of course. You have met Nell. Yet the Director and the Secretary had reached an age when time becomes a glistening factor in the matter of passion. Late blooming indiscretion is not unheard of even in Portland, Oregon, one would hope. And this pair was compatible. Clifford was 46; lean, sinewy, vibrant. Polly was 38; the cold trimness to her basic structure topped off and softened by her playful bosom. She had one of those taut faces that fairly crackles with strident femininity. That trembling racehorse presence that arouses the bronco buster in one. What was our relationship? Should I merely pat her muzzle or should I throw a saddle over the mare?

As I entered the small office, Mrs. Culver cried, "Clifford, thank goodness you came in. I've been trying to reach you at the plant all day. We did it! The Brightwaters School affair. Mathison, that stiff-necked phony, he finally caved in. They want you to speak at the college next Friday."

"Very, very good," I chirped. "If only it had come through sooner..." I told her about my trip to Baltimore. Some of the fizz went out of her but she realigned quickly and said she would get the date pushed back.

"That means you won't make the Boy Scout encampment on the 17th," she said. "Will I, will I, hear from you?"

Ah, my lack of research. Was this the secretary filling out her appointment pad or was this a heartthrob cry from the woman?

"Certainly," I said, "when do you suggest? Naturally, I'll be on the train for four days." (Clifford Waxout had enjoyed a life-long fear of any vehicle that did not maintain contact with the earth; a luxury I envied the gentleman whenever I watched the ground drop away from any airliner I was forced to patronize.)

"I'd love to know what is happening at Middle Atlantic Division," Mrs. Culver said. "Could you possible visit Arlington and find out who they're considering to replace poor Paul Schuh? If it's that man Crossfox...well, I'd be in favor of alerting the FBI to his Montana timber deal. Martin Crossfox is determined to buy his way into the National Directorship. We've got to stop him." Her eyes bobbed in a rolling sea of joyous outrage. Poor Mr. Crossfox. "Can you get over to Arlington?"

"I think so, Polly. Not for the first week or so, though. The mess in Baltimore will tie me down at least that long."

"Baltimore," she said, "a charming city. I'd love to see it again."

What was she saying? Could I just wave goodbye and walk out? Would she detect the uncertainty, the coldness, the imposter?

Come, come, Augustus, when in doubt only a fool doth shirk.

I dropped my hat to a chair and turned toward Polly. Abruptly my attention riveted itself to a section of carpet just below the corner of her desk. "What the heck is that?" I said crossly and walked over and knelt beside the desk.

Mrs. Culver rolled back her chair and leaned her head away trying to view the offending item. Even as I was about my betrayal, my senses were not unalert to the feminine crinkle of her undergarments as she palmed her dress down to cover a pair of succulent knees. I pretended an angry search with my hand of the rug just out of her line of sight. She had no choice but to bend toward me in the chair, her curiosity now strummed to a knife-edge.

"What is it, Cliff?" she asked.

"Take my hand," I said. "I'll show you what it is."

She took the treacherous hand and I pulled her so that she had to bend further from the waist. At this point she was nearly out of the chair. Then, fastening her eyes with mine, I breathed, "My Polly, hold very still just for a moment. Very still, Polly."

Slowly the hand in hers moved toward her. Her eyes, displaying a touching bewilderment, stayed warmly on mine. Almost casually, the fingers of my hand slid like a spider web about the soft thrust of her breast.

"Clifford!" she hissed. Her first instinct was to jerk upright, and then she remembered where we were. Should she sit up we would be in view of the three hacks seated on the other side of the glass partition, a tableau of more than casual interest to the hired help, one supposes.

"Cliff, Cliff, stop it! My God, what's happened to you?" she whispered fiercely. She attempted to draw away the burrowing hand, the five hungry tentacles. There was need to distract her. My other hand, thus far jealously inactive, now skulked into her skirts and raided the soft underside of her thighs. The war on two fronts, not to mention the nibbling rodent teeth that struck at the nape of her scented neck. All in all rather a maximum investigation into her relationship with Clifford Waxout.

Her grip on my wandering hands gradually lost its defensive emphasis; became more a guide to lead me to choice areas. Her voice lost its belligerency. "Clifford, Clifford," she whimpered, "why now? After all these years...why now? Why here?.... Oh you fool, can't we go someplace?...Anyplace. Your office. The basement..."

She was by now out of the chair, crouched with me on the carpet. The Director and the Secretary, a dedicated team once more; ready for sizzling adventure.

"My train leaves in forty minutes," I breathed against her neck.

"My God... But we can't here... Darling, at least let me get this damn girdle out of the way. And for God's sake keep your head down!"

Our parting was one of sworn anguish until I should return. That the reunion would never take place brushed through the halls of my mind and left a trail of sincere regret. The lady had proved capable of furious cooperation. Note the corner of the wall-to-wall carpet, if you will. Ripped from its nailed anchorage during some portion of our engagement.

My march to the corridor door, past the three clerks, was not without dignity. Only the one female of the trio summoned the courage to raise her eye to mine. Her reward was a twinkling leer the unwholesome promise of which drew the blood from her dedicated young face. Yes, my dear, it appears your middle-aged director of Northeast Division is foully human after all.

Speaking of directors and authority and such, one supposes Mrs. Culver was faced with a puzzling problem in office discipline after that day. Polly had kept her eyes closed during the greater part of our affectionate tumble; thus blocking from her fastidious senses the less than romantic commercial fixtures about us. She had missed also the sight of the three hacks coming one at a time for a stricken-eyed gulp of water at the water bottle, which chanced to be positioned adjacent to the glass partition.

Ah well, the critical factor was that the office staff would report, when the time came, that Mr. Waxout's behavior had been unusual, as a matter of fact even slightly abnormal, just prior to his departure for the East Coast.

As I sped toward Seattle that evening in my rented car, I wondered if I should have handled the encounter with Polly somewhat differently. She was to be the key West Coast witness. For my purposes she would report my behavior as flagrantly erratic. Once her inflamed murmurs revealed that my giddy pursuit of her carcass was indeed a unique departure in her association with Clifford Waxout, perhaps I should have, let us say, disengaged, and proceeded out of her office. I daresay that the scar left on her memory would have been somewhat more poignant.

Blast it, no! How many kinds of a cad is a man expected to be?

The final items to detain me, before I took Mr. Waxout from his native city, were dispatched in just twenty minutes. A raid on his safe deposit box put into my greedy note case $15,000.00 in negotiable securities. My hand hovered over the additional $12,000.00 resting in the box, but happily reason rose to slay avarice, I left the poor ownerless notes in their steel grave. Such restraint was certain to impress whichever police body carried the investigation to Portland. Chances are the snoops would be members of the Secret Service since, by jurisdiction, it would be their baby. Still personal discipline of such intensity is not without its price. Thus, when a vice-president of the bank, a Mr. Azzolini, popped from his desk to supply me friendly escort to the front door, I could not restrain my frustration. I found myself snapping loudly, "Never mind, Ozzie, you can't talk me out of it. I'm withdrawing my complete account." He stopped stricken.

At the door of the bank I called back through the crowded lobby, "Tell the board of directors I might reconsider, if they stop betting on those God damn horses. And if they get rid of those flashy girlfriends. Goodbye." Another character reference.

Two blocks from the bank I purchased the gun. It was a .25 caliber with a cold bone handle. Professionally such a miniature weapon is referred to as a 'woman's gun' but when, pray tell, are the dears in season?

Farewell, Portland, Oregon. One of your local lads is off to fame and fortune.

HAVE you ever entertained the thought of doing away with a head of state? Killing off a Prime Minister, say? Or a Premier? A President? A Chairman? Let's say even a King?

I must advise you, my friend, it is not easy. But such assassinations do occasionally take place, so we must conclude that it is always possible.

Library shelves contain very little in the way of guidance or training material on this sort of undertaking. Low demand, I suppose. Therefore, if you are intent on bringing off the event with some degree of success about the only instruction available is in the history of those that have preceded you; the competent and the bunglers.

Those energetic citizens of the United States of America provide us with possibly the most dependable statistics regarding assassination within a modern cultural structure. Then the Americans have always been rather hell bent on providing advice to just about everyone, on just about any subject, particularly to those who have no need for it. Apparently some sort of strong missionary compulsion in their nature.

In the U.S.A. the voters troop to the ballot boxes every four years and elect a fellow citizen to guide them in their pursuit of happiness, tranquility, and their neighbor's goods for the following four years. During this four-year period the gentleman (thus far they have at least had the wisdom to restrict the selection to the male of the species) is known as the President. This President is provided an adequate income, a lovely house for he and his family, painted white and located in Washington D.C. the nation's capital, and a rather disturbing portfolio of powers. Normally the President of the U.S.A. serves his four years with minimum disruption to the nation's equanimity, gets in a satisfying quota of fishing trips or golf dates, and passes on into the history books to befuddle the minds of future school children. There have been times the gentleman may so enchant and/or bamboozle the electorate that they will vote him into office for a second four-year term. One chap was actually voted in four times.

Occasionally this orderly changing of the guard is shattered. Some presidents have died while in office, inducing the disruptive process of changing the identity of the man in the White House. During the first 125 years of the relatively young nation's history, three of its presidents: Lincoln, Garfield, and McKinley left their posts under circumstances that were flagrantly involuntary.

Actually, when one gives it some thought, the incident of presidential assassination in America has been strikingly restrained for so robust a people. In the first 125 years there was but that one short 36-year period in which the citizenry expressed so brazenly its disenchantment with their president: Lincoln in 1865, Garfield in 1882, and McKinley in 1901.

Another 60 years or so were to elapse before another president felt the fatal rebuke of his constituents, Kennedy in 1963. But the events I am so painstakingly weaving in this chronicle took place prior to Mr. Kennedy's embarrassment, thus the judgments provided herein regarding the attempts on the life of a president of the U.S.A., how to go about it, are based on a review of the first three successes. (The properly inquisitive scholar will of course compare my conclusions not only to the results of my own effort in high-level assault but also to the facts in the Kennedy affair.)

When we look at the mechanics of the Lincoln, Garfield, and McKinley episodes we find contained therein rather a primer on successful assassination. For example, in each event the weapon employed was a firearm, a handgun of rather small caliber. The marksmanship, while admittedly effective, was not what one would call first class. Each of the targets lingered on in diminishing health for hours or days following the event.

A rather chilling thought for the Chief Executive one supposes when he ponders that just about any malcontent with even pedestrian eyesight and the price of a bullet is potentially the usher to his grave. About the only consolation to the Chief Executive must lay in the thought that the Americans of late have not taken to the assassination alternative that often.

What is it, would you venture, that caused the secession of presidential bloodletting since that intense period of 36 years when the Americans dismissed one out of every three from the office by lead poisoning? Temerity among the peasants? I think not. Where you have an efficient workable society there you will have also your anarchist, if only for sentiment's sake.

The answer, I believe, is associated with the advent of amplified communication. There has come to the comfort of the despot the cold microphone that flings his voice outward while maintaining a non-aggressor buffer zone between his carcass and the trigger-happy. The President of the U.S.A. has become almost inaccessible during 3½ of the 4 years he is in office. During the remaining ½ year of course, those preceding the rearing up of the implacable ballot box, he must turn gregarious. He must tuck his head in the muck and swirl it about, his teeth naked in nailed mirth, his convictions of superiority chained in leg irons deep in his craw.

The evidence, dear student, indicates that ballistic insult is visited on the man from the White House most successfully when he overestimates his rapport with the voters. To mingle with your electorate is to court your reaper. Mr. Garfield was walking through a railroad station when the viper struck. Mr. McKinley was actually standing in the open, greeting and shaking the hands of his constituents when he chanced upon one Leon Czolgesz, a sorehead whose salutation betrayed his gross incivility. Mr. Lincoln was seated in a public theater.

Now there is a gathering of brave ruffians who are charged with protecting the epidermis of the Chief Executive from dents, gashes, holes, contusions, clots and fractures. They are members of the Secret Service, the President's bodyguard, and they are as aware of the incident of distress inherent in public exposure of the Chief as you and I, more so it is hoped. These burly guardians focus a thoughtful barrage of precaution toward absolving the man from the White House of physical damage during his fresh-air appearances. By statistic they must be credited with uncommon success. They have not lost that many presidents. As a matter of fact the record of diligence displayed by the Secret Service would cause an alert assassin to conclude that he would be challenging rather stringent rebuttal were he to commit himself during an occasion when his target is apparently "open to the public."

Let's see what we have thus far?

1. The weapon: Handgun, small. The selection of any alternate device is unsupported by research.
2. Distance from target: Very close; dictated by the range of the weapon and, again, by the lack of any evidence that the microphone barrier can be overcome.
3. Occasion: Semi-private exposure of the target. The assassins of Garfield and McKinley, who selected an open-air arena for their antics, were seized immediately. Mr. Booth appears to have put a bit of thought into his dispute with President Lincoln, at least in regard to establishing an appropriate exit (he had been trained in Theater.) Thus, he enjoyed a period of unrestricted movement following the event.

All right, my amateur assassins let us apply ourselves to this issue of "Occasion;" reason it down to some size one can lay hold of. We seek a semi-private audience with the Chief Executive. That objective requires that we select an hour when the gentleman is available either during his business affairs or during his social life.

To reach the president during his business day requires in essence that you be escorted to his office or that you gain entrance to a room that he will visit, a conference or meeting room. This approach is open to exploitation. I mean there are any number of groups before which the President presents petitions of presumed interest to the voters: a gathering of governors, congressmen, diplomats, generals and admirals, businessmen, all sorts of clutches.

But an attack during office hours includes a peril any competent assassin will refuse to enjoin. The alertness of the Secret Servicemen on these occasions is only slightly less severe than that in force during the public appearances. The chance of being apprehended immediately following your labor is scandalous. Of course if your motive is but to exhibit your fanaticism, if you are prepared to receive in proportion to that which you have delivered, this restriction will not matter. You deserve everything you get, you crackpot.

Thus: for he who hopes to promote the demise of the Chief Executive and survive to wallow in the material gains thereof (the fee) the inescapable favorite as to time and place is to be found in the President's social schedule. Take your choice: a ball, a party, a dinner. Since the guest lists for such affairs are considered to include the irreproachable, if only because they reflect the Chief's taste, the security arrangements are less awesome. If one could arrange to be included on such a guest list, and one arrived at the affair with a small caliber pistol secreted on one's person, why one could rather have his way.

As I said, doing away with a head of state is not a simple matter. But, my friend, which of the worthwhile endeavors in this life is?

Have you ever heard of the firm of Mandrell Limited? Chances are your answer is 'no.' Do not let it disturb you. Our clientele is decidedly select and we do not advertise. Oddly enough there is still room in the commercial arena for such a firm despite your interlocking corporations and the million dollar advertising budgets. Then, there is always a market for excellence.

I am Augustus Mandrell, the founder, president, chief executive, principal employee, and treasurer—yes, quite definitely the Treasurer—of the firm. We do employ others occasionally but they are chaps of unique talents and once we have utilized the talent we generally arrange a separation based on mutual agreement; or not based on mutual agreement. I leave it up to the employee. Such a policy markedly reduces our retirement overhead: parties, gifts, stock options, lingering payrolls; all of those offensive long-term charity factors of modern business.

Ours is a service organization. The service itself is rather difficult to describe; I mean to describe with all of its subtle ramifications. If you insist on one of those terse explanations, gross terminology designed for quick reading by your ever so busy executive, "maximum elucidation with minimum exposition"—isn't that what you call it? –another soul-less efficiency inflicted upon us by commercial Man's illogical conclusion that "higher speed means higher profit", or, in terms of the wisdom harvested by the generals from two World Wars: "Higher speed means higher killing rate"—anyway, if it is the quick resume you demand you shall have it: The firm of Mandrell Limited is in the business of insuring that selected individuals move from this life on to the next life not on a schedule arranged by Mother Nature or by mischance but rather on a schedule dictated by an "interested party" (my customer.)

It is as simple as that, old man. Should you wish to tamper with a loved one's residency on this planet, why Mandrell Limited is at your service. But, my dear chap, I must emphasize, and re-emphasize, do not come to us unless you have appreciation for the price of excellence (the fee.) Do not be misled by your exposure to a marketplace where slipshod products and practices have achieved the esteem we once reserved for "adequate" and adequate has been elevated to the rank of "outstanding" and outstanding is never heard of any more.

Mandrell Limited, as I mentioned, deals in excellence. The firm, in its own small way, is attempting to restore craftsmanship in a world where this honest term is known in legend only. While any hackneyed firm can initiate an illusion of quality by simply attaching an outrageous price tag to its product—automobile manufacturers and jewelers are particularly adroit at this sort of flim flam—the firm of Mandrell Limited assesses the worth of its service and establishes its fees in consonance with a very realistic baseline. Permit me to put it this way: we are far and away the "best in the business."

But if you are an astute shopper you will certainly not accept my rather prejudiced estimate. I would not in your place. Let us then look at testimonial from a source that has, over the years, had cause to evaluate my competitors and myself. Let us look at a portion of the report from Scotland Yard regarding an affair called The Fighter Pilot's Ghost Commission..

The chaps at the Yard have maintained a rather touching interest in my affairs ever since The Doctor Sherrock Commission—ah, so many years ago, Augustus—and are therefore probably the best qualified of the world's policing establishments to offer a judgment. (Do I detect a murmur of dissent from the Mexico City Police Department?) Anyway, this is how the Yard investigator put it: (Incidentally, Gentlemen, I must compliment you on the ventilation system installed in your Priority Security Records Division. During my five hours of foraging the files, 1:00 AM to 6:00 AM, I did not have to remove even my suit jacket.)

Part 111 Paragraph 6: The suspect, Augustus Mandrell, is rather well known to Yard personnel. He has plied his ghastly trade here and on the Continent for an embarrassing number of years. (See file drawers 36 through 41) The fact that suspect, Mandrell, employs a number of disguises is, in the opinion of this office, a frail excuse for the failure of the Criminal Investigation Division (CID) to apprehend the suspect..."

Scotland Yard management has been notably unsuccessful in persuading their individual divisions to refrain from issuing these personalized judgments. Admittedly such comments have no place in an official police report. Pursue sometime the terse, phlegmatic reports of the West German Policing establishment. Now there's a group of chaps who know how to present boggling detail with parade ground precision. Left foot, right foot, forward, march, and a jolly snap into it. Good form, all right. But then perhaps it is precisely this peculiarly British human touch, this refusal to submerge the ego that has always endeared the chaps at Scotland Yard to so many; those that have never dealt with them directly.

The report goes on:

Part 111 Paragraph 7: There is ample evidence to conclude that this man Mandrell was the direct agent in the murder of a Superintendent of Scotland Yard. Despite the conclusion to the contrary by the Home Office and even other, shall we say, "short-sighted" divisions within our own establishment, this office firmly believes that Augustus Mandrell murdered Sir Bruce Peak in Toulon, France in 1944. Admittedly, Mr. Mandrell was seen in London early on the morning following Sir Bruce's death, but this office feels it unwarranted to assume Mandrell could not have made his way 600 miles from Toulon to London in the interim. For God's sake, World War II was on. There was any number of high-speed military aircraft available! Has any agency thought to examine the records for reports of pilfered aircraft in the area of Toulon on that evening? Has any official bestirred himself to conduct even the preliminary research to determine if one Augustus Mandrell has ever been issued a flight certificate? A pilot's license? God damn it, sir, the man may have even been a member of the Royal Air Force at some time or other! Wasn't Lawrence of Arabia? The life of a Scotland Yard Super has been taken!"

While I am receptive to the inclusion of personal commentary in official reports, those occasional sparks of individualism that ignite so delightfully in the midst of the dull gray cobblestones of bureaucratic language, I'm afraid I must concur that it can be carried to excess. Hysteria is hardly the sort of thing to promote interoffice harmony.

But now we get to the meat of the Scotland Yard report. Incidentally, for those of you who did not attend a first rank university (Cambridge, say; or even Boston) and thus were served your introduction to English Literature by some musty chap with a hunched back mind, if this indeed was your fate then in all probability you are having difficulty grasping the slippery bits and pieces provided in the above extract regarding the demise of Scotland Yard Superintendent Sir Bruce Peak. Happily a fuller account of the affair is available and, in those countries where the document is no longer classified as CONFIDENTIAL, FOR OFFICIAL USE ONLY, you can normally find the account on the shelves of almost any decent library. The document is titled, The Scotland Yard Commission, and is judged to be unimpeachably authentic. It was penned by my own hand you see.

Now, as I said, 'the meat' of this other document, which, as you must have gathered, was not issued by the Criminal Investigation Division (CID) there at the Yard. The memo was signed out by someone in the Budget and Accounting Office (BAO) oddly enough.

<u>Part 111 Paragraph 8:</u> While we have been assured by CID (his memo of 17 Aug.) that, quote: "exhaustive pursuit of suspect Augustus Mandrell has been discharged" unquote, this office takes exception to CID's interpretation of the term, "...exhaustive pursuit." Dispatching two Chief Inspectors to Toronto, Canada dur-

ing the subject investigation and from thence to Chicago, Illinois, U.S.A. and Mexico City, Mexico could certainly be termed "pursuit" were there any evidence that suspect Mandrell had been at any of these localities at the time. There is no such evidence. There is only the empty cell here in London at Metro Police Headquarters where Mr. Mandrell was to take residence.

Part 111, Paragraph 9: Does CID take us for buffoons? "...exhaustive pursuit?" While it may not have been "pursuit" it was certainly "exhaustive" in terms of depleting our financial resources. Two round trip air fares; sixteen, repeat sixteen, days of Subsistence and Allowance for two Chief Inspectors; nine days in which the CID's Chief Inspectors carried out their "exhaustive pursuit" in rental automobiles; six trans-Atlantic telephone calls (to report what? weather conditions? certainly not success.) A grand total expenditure of £528 pounds sterling." (Approximately $2,100.00 dollars, my American readers.)

The figure would have been even more staggering had it not been for the generosity of our brother officials of the Royal Canadian Mounted Police. While RCMP could not quite see their way clear to provide petrol they did put a vehicle at the disposal of CID's two Chief Inspectors. Thus a rental car was not required. The cooperative gentlemen of the Mexico City Police Department also showed an awareness of fiscal responsibility in this transportation issue. At least they offered our lads a 1936 Dodge from their repository of Unclaimed Vehicles. Chief Inspector Kevin Hanley notes in his Expenditure Voucher that he declined the Mexican conveyance because, quote: "...the ruddy thing was as full of bullet holes as a Swiss cheese. Hardly an official-appearing vehicle..." unquote. It is the fond hope of this office that Chief Inspector Hanley's alternate choice, the rented American Chrysler, initiated the sought-for response from the smouldering Mexico City senoritas.

Gentlemen of the Mexico City Police Dept., how touching. You retain still the machine that brought us together? A 1936 Dodge riddled with bullets, surely it is the same vehicle? I must confess, your sentimental gesture slightly embarrasses me. My English reserve, you know.

Enough of this maudlin pap, Augustus. Wipe away that tear and press on to the reality of the Scotland Yard Budget and Accounting Office memo.

"...In Chicago, Illinois, U.S.A. our high living travelers encountered no mention of supplemental transportation from the police of that community. And, one must suspect our, shall we say, rather spoiled Chief Inspectors probably did not encourage any such consideration on the part of the Chicago police. During the Audit Hearings, Chief Inspector Hanley put it thus, "Subject never came up. American law enforcers appear to regard ownership of an automobile as some sort of birthright. In that strange country one is immediately suspected of Communism and the like if one is not continually complaining of traffic congestion, parking shortages, and decaying chrome trim." One would be tempted to accept the Chief Inspector's analysis of the American policing mind with a firm, "here, here" if one did not have a bit of knowledge regarding the condition of the vehicle the Royal Canadian Mounted Police provided our two Chief Inspectors. Chief Inspector Hanley's companion in this inter-continental (let us say "expedition", calling it an "official investigation" would be in the view of this office, a diluting of the business-like quality of the latter term) anyway, Chief Inspector, Michael King was the other half of the team. Chief Inspector King is quoted by one of his staff (more correctly, a former member of his staff) as having passed the following judgment regarding the RCMP loan vehicle:

"It was a right enough auto for moving about the countryside. I mean the engine would ignite and the tires held the ruddy thing off the roadway, and all that. But the passenger seat backrest was broken; meaning one of us was continually riding in the backseat where the springs came through the cushions. And you know the type Kevin is." (Chief Inspector Kevin Hanley) "He insisted on doing all the driving even though his touch with a road map isn't what you'd call awe inspiring. Thought for a while there we'd spend the rest of our lives in the back streets of Toronto making one wrong turn after another." The notes here on Chief Inspector King's remarks indicate that the several members of the Chief Inspector's staff present at the "debriefing" (held in a private bar at the Rudder Room) "laughed heartily." Chief Inspector King has since denied making some of the remarks attributed to him. But the former member of his staff who submitted the report to this office, with a "further transmittal" to Superintendent Boyle of CID, claims with convincing vehemence that he composed his notes there on the spot at the Rudder Room (or at least, in the men's lavatory of the Rudder Room) on the night in question.

Part 111, Paragraph 10:

The fact remains that our two Chief Inspectors were less than enchanted with the RCMP vehicle and took to themselves a rental auto in the city of Chicago, a Chrysler no less. No economical "British import" for our lads on American soil, no indeed. A Department Directive titled "Foreign Travel; Permissible Expenses Associated With" has been drafted and submitted to Head for his signature.

Part 111, Paragraph 11:

While it is hardly the function of this office to advise other divisions of their, shall we say, "shortcomings," we would feel derelict in duty were we not to point out to all concerned that this person Augustus Mandrell is still at large. That Mr. Mandrell is a match for any single brain within our investigative divisions appears obvious. Does it then follow that this assassin par excellence is a match for the whole of the Yard? This office feels it's high time we put an end to Augustus Mandrell's monstrous career and return to a policy of fiscal sanity.

Part 111, Paragraph 12:

Request for additional file drawer in which to house the expanding dossier of one Mandrell, Augustus is denied.

End of memo.

There was little in the Scotland Yard files to indicate the internal reaction to the Budget and Accounting Office memo. One short memo from CID dated the following day was stapled to the back of the BAO memo. The CID memo said simply "Your memo of the 24th reviewed. Concur on several points, in particular Part 111, Paragraph 9, first sentence."

So there you have it, Ladies and Gentlemen. Scotland Yard has chosen to rate the firm of Mandrell Limited as, "par excellence." Surely we must concede that they are in a position to know about such things. The Yard and I, we have had our little tiffs, admittedly, but even in the Law and Order business, an Englishman's innate sense of sportsmanship and fair play cannot be submerged indefinitely.

Therefore I point out that the considerations, which govern the establishing of a Mandrell Unlimited fee, are based on the quality of the service, kindly refrain from skepticism.

Our credentials are not only impeccable; they are a matter of public record.

Leaving Portland, Oregon, I was impressed with an economical view of the Willamette River teeming with those feats of engineering delight...bridges. All of which connect the west side of Portland (where Clifford's pleasant, albeit stout wife, Nell, remained oblivious to his recent occupation of a rather saline tenement. Ah, but the groupers do so enjoy your company, lad!) with the east side of Portland (this being the location of the seventh floor love nest of the toothsome Polly Culver.) Were it ever in the stars for these two women to perhaps be out walking (not a religious habit of Nell's I'm afraid) and chance to meet while navigating one such bridge, well, I'm afraid the results would be fraught with the emotional clap-trap associated with the comparing-of-notes in which the female species is so inclined to indulge. Ah, but chance is grounded in the mathematics of probability and the odds were in my favor that they would not, under happenstance, meet. I believe there are a few chaps in the fine city of Las Vegas who have made a tidy living out of just such a notion.

The aircraft had only one short layover in Chicago and proceeded on to the east coast with a new crop of lovely stewardesses and eventually I was released from its aluminum viscera at the Newark, New Jersey airport. Odd city Newark. It apparently has never felt the desire to flaunt its own obvious charm, preferring instead to tremble with coquettish docility beneath the giant brooding thumb of New York City just across the river.

The next morning I was in Washington, D.C. or, should one consult the proper hotel register, Clifford Waxout was in Washington, D.C. Haste was in order. The dispatching of the real Clifford Waxout in the state of Oregon had taken a bit more time than I had scheduled. The completion of The President's Poverty Commission was to take place in just three weeks. In those weeks I had to win from one of the world's most beautiful women her trust, her admiration, a portion at least of her love, and in all probability her chastity. As I had yet to meet the maid, obviously I would have to dispense with some of the more subtle cape work normally employed in these commissions. Ah well, the only chap to suffer would be the maitre d' at Whitman's.

He was at his post when I entered the restaurant at 11:45 AM. Beyond his velvet rope the higher income citizens of the United States' "Federal Community" in Washington, D.C.: the senators, cabinet members, senior State Dept. personnel, lobbyists, and the like, were seated at the 100 or so tables ordering their pre-lunch cocktails. The three middle-aged musicians on the small bandstand located in the center of the dining room were equipped with violins only. No recorded music at Whitman's and definitely no vulgar brass instruments.

Eventually those expensively dressed gentlemen and expensively scented maids in line before me were moved on to tables by the crisp maitre d'. He had excellent teeth and a rapier-like smile; they are handed out by the Academy at graduation, as I understand it.

"I'd like to have a table close to Miss DiMartino's," I whispered to the maitre d'.

He turned his head to look out over the dining room, at his prosperous farm where his gold-jacketed field hands were tenderly cultivating the neat rows of ripe tables. It was the time of the luncheon harvest. "Ah, Monsieur," he answered, "the only table available in zat vicinity, it ez for a party of four. Zum one will join you?"

"I'd *very* much like a table near Miss DiMartino," I said.

"Ah.Monsieur. Come this way please."

When I look back on it I believe the breakdown in communication between the maitre d' and myself took place during that exchange. I had merely voiced a particular desire. Later the events indicate the maitre d' had attached to my simple words some subterranean sophistication far beyond my intent. The language barrier perhaps.

I was seated within 20 paces of Miss DiMartino and her three luncheon companions; all three male.

Consuela DiMartino. Consuela. Consuela.

You must admit, sir, Mother Nature does have a conscience. She normally will go on year after year serving up human beings at what might be considered an injudicious rate. Can she be blamed if in this flurry of mass production there is a diminishing attention to quality? Yet, every once in a while our good Mother will pause, reflect, remorse, possibly even go back to the drawing board. She must, after all, have her pride. She will look about. She will shudder at the sight of such a volume of slops. A period of contrition will set in and she will strive for atonement. She will, from some hidden recess of her loins, pluck forth a single, jewel-like individual and stand that individual on the earth before us, before our awe and consternation. Perhaps it is that our dear Mother is only about the business of proving that she doesn't need, and will not brook with, any advice or interference from her upstart children, those mad scientist chaps in the labs with their ruddy test tubes and theories regarding genetics.

Thus I do rate The DiMartino; one of Mom's gifts to we assembly line products.

Miss DiMartino, among her other virtues, was a person of schedule. When in the Eastern Time Zone of the United States she lunched precisely at 11:30 AM when she was in Washington, D.C. she lunched always at Whitman's, and sat invariably at table 27. Thus, were I to steal from this much pursued lady (amorously speaking) those rather personal possessions I have already itemized, I was decidedly in the proper location, table 28.

During our first encounter, with the width of a serving aisle separating us, I limited our intimacy to a static observation of the lady by myself. I knew much about the DiMartino, as of course do we all, but I had never met her. I found myself strangely relieved to discover that my second-hand enchantment with the dame was not diluted during the luncheon encounter.

The beauty was even more striking than the color photos had indicated. The poise, as she and the three gentlemen with her chatted through lunch, was even more pronounced than the television screen had projected. The carriage, as she rose and exited the restaurant, was of an assurance that bordered on the regal. And the moving parts that supported the carriage—my God, Augustus, the lady is a delight!

As I entered Whitman's on the second day of my...er...attack, I perceived that there was to be some unpleasantness with the maitre d'. The man had his self-respect I suppose. Still I would have thought that he would have also the wit to recognize that retreat in the face of a superior contestant is in itself a type of victory, not to mention common sense. Ah well.

As I suspected, the maitre d' and I had not communicated adequately during my first visit the previous day. I had obtained the table I requested. The maitre d' had not obtained whatever it was his mean ambitions expected from me. We must of course ponder the man's lack of proper timing. If he had anticipated remuneration for his kindness to me, why, the man should have spoken up prior to seating me. His bargaining power after that was certainly not as effective as it had been. He was not one of your "slow learners" however. Following my lunch on that first day, as I exited past the maitre d's unobstructive palm, leaving therein only the warmth of my curt nod, the fellow had unleashed a glare upon me of considerable voltage. It was certainly not the sort of adieu a maitre d' extends a well-qualified customer.

And so, on the second day there was a spark of anticipation when his eyes glanced toward the entrance and struck mine and he recognized me. Revenge has always had its meaty side. But, my dear chap, this is the second skirmish. The ground rules are different.

I was past the orderly line of waiting diners and past the maitre d's contemptuous lip before it occurred to the man that I was not about to stop at his velvet barrier. I had stepped over the rope and was well on to table 28 before the gentleman's senses could bring his cavalry about to defend his flank.

Of course he followed me into the room and delivered into my ear some rather pedestrian commands. The ear he found to be infuriatingly porous. His disposition was decidedly uncivil. I, for instance, was forced to adjust my own chair as I took my seat at table 28.

My adversary was not without resources however. He signaled two waiters and, shielding his venom behind his wine list, ordered his lads to remove from the room the table at which I sat. The obedient coolies went about the task briskly but with a high sense that adjacent diners were not to be alerted to the in-fighting. They quickly snatched the floral centerpiece and my linen napkin and were about the business of gathering the silverware. High time to bring in our fusiliers, eh, what, Colonel? Right you are, sir.

"On second thought," I announced to the maitre d' in a voice pitched several decibels above the mean din in the surrounding area. "On second thought, leave the table where it stands. It has just occurred to me that the other spot is rather too adjacent to the scullery door. More the location for the representative from the Health Department, wouldn't you say? Ho, ho, ho..."

Ah, but an ambush is a pretty thing to watch.

The shocked eyes of the maitre d' surveyed the battlefield. The two waiters had frozen in their tracts. To continue with the removal of the table, it was now obvious, meant involving the awareness of the credit card customers who were beginning to turn their eyes to table 28. Also, my reference to the Health Department carried with it its own explosive mechanism. The carefully chosen words indicated that I would be rather without delicacy, were the altercation to continue.

The maitre d' fell back to his second redoubt. To his minions he whispered fiercely, "Leave it. Zare will be no service at zis table until this....this specimen departs." His "about face," executed with military precision on a single leather heel, remains to this day a benchmark against which all such exits are measured.

"Ah yes, Eric," I called lustily to the departing waiter (he had sufficiently calculated the previous day to drop his name upon me with the menu,) "The fried calf's liver again, if you please, Eric. And do, old boy, try to fetch it this time prior to the congealing of the onions to the surface of the plate."

Eric and the maitre d' continued their stiff retreat without turning, the backs of their necks quite red.

I glanced about at my attentive fellow diners and triggered their sympathy with the helplessness of my shrug and my *c'est la guerre* mein.

Evidently the maitre d' was determined to enforce the embargo. Even my appalled sniffing and peering down the spout of the water carafe drew no fire. I found it necessary to accidentally tip the water vessel on to the carpeted floor where it rolled into a position to impede the passage of waiters and guests and spilled its contents. A scout was sent forth into no man's land, a bus boy with a sponge.

As the lad finished mopping the rug I addressed him, "Son,

would you be good enough to tell the manager I wish to speak to him. My billfold appears to be missing." My voice carried my note of concern to the ears of several adjacent tables. "I believe the maitre d' removed it from my pocket," I continued. "Possibly by accident."

The lad said, "Yes, sir." and was about to dash off with the empty water carafe.

"Take care with that vessel," I advised the youth. "Do not permit the contents to come in contact with your skin." As he moved off, I called in a stage whisper that carried well into the room. "In particular do not touch that greenish substance there about the neck of the jar."

Miss Consuela DiMartino's table was directly in my line of sight. Her chair faced mine. The same three male companions from the previous day were with her again. While they had their own interests to occupy them they had kept a portion of their attention on the duel in progress between myself and the staff of Whitman's. They were civilized people and had the wit to recognize the element of humor in the affair.

The man at their table with his back directly toward me, handsome chap with a good neck, turned in his seat and grinned at me. "Nice going, pal," he said. "I think you've got them."

And who are you, sir, to intrude yourself into my affairs? I stared back at him with cold affront until he turned away embarrassed and childishly angry. Miss DiMartino laughed easily then put her hand over the man's and murmured something.

As I said, Miss Di Martino's chair faced mine. Any other arrangement made no sense, don't you see?

When her eye encountered mine following the rebuff of her friend, there was interest in it. My returning stare told her only that I considered her a strikingly lovely woman. It did not tell her that I also knew her to be the finest soprano who had ever drawn a breath on the stage at La Scala. Such lack of recognition was calculated to pique the diva, to arouse a level of curiosity in her concerning this self-possessed fellow diner with his harsh rimless glasses and great expanse of baldness above them, a nudity of scalp disguised by naught but a scattering of uncompromising freckles. A man of the world, no doubt about it.

Ah, my Consuela, keep those frank green eyes on table 28 now. This midget war, this manipulation of complacent egos, it is for you, my sweet.

Across the room at the velvet rope a portly figure of authority in a seersucker suit was in conference with the maitre d'. The overweight gentleman was annoyed and as they spoke his glaring searchlight eye swept several times out over the room to hold me momentarily in its beam. The young man with the water carafe had carried the message to headquarters.

The maitre d' was providing the general from headquarters a resume of the skirmishes to date. The suave gentleman (the maitre d') had beautifully articulate hands. The manager's hands remained in the side pockets of his suit jacket curled into fists. As he listened to his maitre d' his face reflected the degree of sympathy one associates with a tarantula.

About time to lie on a bit of artillery, eh wot Sergeant Major?

I stood up at my table and lifted the tablecloth of eye-catching white linen high toward the ceiling. Any who cared to observe the sideshow then saw me peering worriedly at the floor under the table. At the same time my free hand patted my suit pockets obviously in search of some item. Fully three quarters of the diners were now caught up in near silent absorption with the drama.

"What does one do?" I was heard to ask those seated in my area. "The police...?"

The manager himself chose to deliver the capitulation. He of course had been least bloodied in the encounter.

"Please be seated," he whispered upon arriving at my table. "You will be served immediately." He then flattened against my supercilious face his most lethal glare. "As soon as you have eaten—get out," he hissed. "And don't come back—ever!"

He was about to demonstrate his "about face" (not realizing, perhaps that his maitre d' had given him a very hard act to follow.) I sighed and said, "I suppose I am hardly in a position to comment on the...ah, *service* since it appears I have misplaced my notecase." I had determined that an indemnity was in order.

The manager blinked with a lack of comprehension. He turned and started walking away.

"Evidently you didn't hear me," I called after him. "The check, I'll be forced to sign for it. And, since my only identification was in my wallet—"

"For God's sake, have the waiter bring it to me," he cried and fled past the tables back to some world he understood.

The lunch was excellent. Consuela's eye drifted to me several times. On the first of our eye contacts the dear thing even passed me a very slight smile of congratulations. My responding nod could not have been colder. I'll have none of your childish hero worship, madam.

I left Whitman's feeling rather smug with the progress of The President's Poverty Commission. How quickly our gluttonous egos are appeased. Even the simple matter of 'beating a man at his own game' contains sufficient nourishment to sustain a small inner flame of contentment. We are but adolescents after all.

But, Augustus, one does not progress on minor victories. The real general, my son, is he who accepts nothing from the enemy but total surrender. I have the impression, mon general, that the staff at Whitman's feels they still retain a major portion of their strength and are prepared to do battle once more. Impertinent lot.

As I entered Whitman's at 11:45 AM on the third day I presumed there would be anti-social display or other. I was not disappointed.

The manager and the maitre d' were both on hand at the velvet barrier. I suspect that while their instinct for combat was by this time at some flammable level or other their pragmatic sense told them they would see no more of the boor, that I would not dare return. Gentlemen, do not despair. Circumstances require that I be seated in the vicinity of Consuela DiMartino one more time.

The backs of the maitre d' and the manager were to me as I approached the roadblock. They were watching the front entrance, you see, and I had entered through the kitchen. I stood behind them for a moment, and then cleared my throat politely.

"My same table, if you please," I said. "I believe it is number 28."

It was the manager who chose to raise the lance. "That table is taken," he snapped. "And so are all the others as far as you are concerned."

I moved a step to the side so that my voice should reach the outer rim of diners.

"Yes," I said in a puzzled, clear voice, "that is true, I am Jewish."

It was obvious from the menu that Whitman's devoted about one quarter of its kitchen to indulging in the Judaic pallet, a bonus for the discerning Gentile gourmets.

"I didn't say anything about being Jewish," the manager hissed, cornering his eyes about wildly to discover if I had been overheard.

My shoulders went slack, my head bowed a bit. While my voice still carried well, it was now aimed at the manager's shoes. "I see. If that is Whitman's policy...of course I'll leave quietly. Could you... would you be kind enough to recommend a restaurant where I will be served?"

"Get out! Get out of here, you lunatic!" His voice writhed in fury but it was held audible to myself only since it was processed through his clenched teeth.

"I see," I said sadly and my posture sunk deeper into my mantle of persecution. "If you can't serve even some of your best friends... but about another restaurant, one that is not restricted? Perhaps one of your patrons would know..." I leaned slightly over the flower-decorated grill divider toward the outer perimeter of tables.

"You could pardon the intrusion, please?" I said to the staring diners, "A stranger I am in this Washington city. You could tell me maybe where there is a restaurant where they will serve a—"

"Your table will be ready in a moment, sir," the manager's booming voice announced. He took my arm in a fierce grip and held me while the maitre d' fumbled open the velvet rope. "The gentleman's usual table, Marcel," the manager said, releasing me to the custody of the maitre d'.

"I hope you enjoy your lunch, sir," the manager said, his voice indicating not at all that its hospitality was so newly minted. His eyes, however, shivered in his head and he had a parting whisper for me. "We'll see you when you get ready to leave, you son of a bitch."

As the tight-lipped maitre d' led me past Miss DiMartino's table, I noted that she had before her usual spare lunch: onion soup, cottage cheese, and fresh pear slices. There was a moment's pause at her table while the governor of New Mexico and three young ladies wearing Indian beaded dresses were seated at table 30. The dark-eyed governor insisted on personally seating his guests. In the process he managed a lingering glance down the v-shaped neckline of each of the maids; an inquiry the political overtones of which escaped me.

During the pause Miss DiMartino slid her forthright eyes up to mine and said, "I see you made it again."

"Certainly, Madam," I replied coolly. "A man has to eat, unfortunately."

Her interest could not have been more timely. I glanced at her hand, at the diamond ring on the middle finger. "Ahh, such excellence," I murmured. "Permit me..." I grasped the hand before she had time to protest and lifted it to line my eye on the ring.

"Too bad, too bad," I mumbled a judgment. "But to be expected. Such inner frigidity, the cold blue, is almost always flawed by those warm highlights. Too bad..."

"I presume you are speaking of the stone, sir," she said, amused, "and not the owner?" The hand rested easily in mine, yet with the fine body tremble that invades those who lead a high voltage life.

"Huh?" I said as though startled to discover that the hand belonged to someone. "Oh, yes, yes, of course," I said absently. I dropped the fingers impersonally and moved on to take the chair being held for me by my friend, Marcel.

Miss DiMartino and her companions, the same three gentlemen, did not miss the gesture in which I idly wiped on my jacket the hand that had held hers. A sharp intake of breath was audible from one gentleman. They did not miss this insult but had they been more observant they would have noted that as my hand moved over Consuela's cup of onion soup it had deposited therein a small chemical pellet.

As I waited for my own order of onion soup to arrive I observed contentedly the gusto with which the slightly annoyed diva devoured hers. When my soup did arrive I polluted it also with the same chemical, although it probably contained the contamination already. On my entrance through the kitchen, you see, I had popped several of the pellets into a simmering cauldron of the same.

A few minutes after being served I summoned my waiter, the dour Eric. "What in God's name is in this soup?" I asked crossly. "What is that reddish discoloration?"

"It looks alright to me, sir," he joyfully lied.

"Having tasted the beverage," I said a bit louder, "I can assure you it is not *all right*." I sniffed at a spoonful. "The damn thing smells like..." I sniffed some more. "Yes, damn it. It's ARSENIC! The ruddy Lucrezia Borgia strain, unless I miss my guess."

I glanced around wildly. "Good God, man, have you served any more of this POISON?"

I was on my feet by then. Very near the opposite was true of poor Eric. The adjacent area was well alerted. Heads had popped to attention as the sensitive gizzards in the room shied and reared from the blood-drenched words: arsenic, Borgia, poison.

I stepped quickly to a table at which sat a man with decently manicured hands and a thin woman with a collar of tier upon tier of pearls. The man had a half empty cup of onion soup on his plate.

I snatched the cup and poured its contents into the floral centerpiece. "High yourself off to your physician instantly, you idiot," I snarled. "You've been POISONED!"

The hot beverage had a predictable and rather picturesque affect on the wax-based clutch of vegetation in the centerpiece. The flowers—peonies, as I recall—shuddered, bent, and one by one began dropping from their crystal bowl to the tabletop. The thin woman stared at the disintegration with, I presume, horror. Her facial skin quickly attained a yellowish cast that actually complimented and made almost acceptable the deluge of pearls clutching her epiglottis.

Now, Augustus, now! Three days of exquisite timing dancing on the tip of one split second of action.

I spun to the table where sat my quarry, my treasure. Slamming the palm of my hand over the mouth of the soup cup in front of Consuela DiMartino, I glared at her with Jehovistic accusation. "You drank this?" I roared.

Her nod was a response by instinct.

"Do you need a God damn drawing?" I screeched at her three companions. "This woman is POISONED! At this very minute her throat is being eaten by ACID!" -- Ah, but didn't that hit the opera star's friends like a mailed fist.

"Quick, get some of this into her immediately." On the back of one of my business cards I scrawled: Olive oil. Milk. Mixed. "Hurry you fools, hurry," I croaked as I stuffed the card into the dumbfounded hand of Monsieur Pierre Brichant who I knew to be her manager. The other two men, Jeremy Beushausen, the conductor, and Scott Valboa, the DiMartino's companion and probably her lover, were already at Consuela's side helping her from her chair.

"You should find those ingredients in the kitchen...gah." My voice had become noticeably strangled. As I tore away my tie, I gasped, "After she vomits...Gah...get her to...to a doctor."

I staggered back against my table, overturning it. "As for me... Gah...I'm afraid I may have had it..."

I stumbled blindly toward the rear of the room. At each table I passed I attempted to support my mortally wounded body by grasping the tablecloth. The anchorage was of course insufficient. I succeeded only in stripping the linen from the tables, along with dishes and other items sitting thereon. Multitudes were on their feet by this time. My reeling body was uncontrollable. My shoulder came up under the arm of several chaps, those of sufficient bulk to generate the more alarming demolition, and pitched them onto adjacent tables or neighboring diners.

As I negotiated the fire exit and stumbled into the alley beyond, an avant-garde symphony roared to life in my wake. The cymbals were adequately replaced by splintering, crashing china; the brass by the sharp complaints of trampled, wounded silverware; the kettle drums by the demonic howls of female diners; their natural talent brought to fortissimo perfection by scalded thighs under soup-splashed skirts.

It was a day in the history of Whitman's Restaurant to be recalled only by those employees possessed of cast iron gall.

The aftermath fell like stones in a mosaic.

The "poison" was actually a rather docile concoction. It induced a short period of cramps, the severity of which served but to remind the stomach to be on its toes that less considerate diets than those indulged in by Americans do exist.

Miss DiMartino was out of the hospital by the next morning. Her voice regained its full awesome power within a week, a period during which her psychiatrist finally convinced her that the other quack, her medical doctor, spoke the truth regarding the absence of damage to her priceless throat.

The other patrons of Whitman's—a total of seven were the recipients of my culinary innovation—recuperated as lustily and only six of these sued the establishment.

As for myself, well I had evidently quaffed an overdose. I languished in the hospital for a full three days, creating a minor medical mystery actually. The wild fluctuations of my temperature (child's play) had the staff thumbing their reference books far into the night. I did not really get back on my feet until after the visit from Monsieur Pierre Brichant who brought to me a summary of his client's gratitude. The portly manager had traced me through my hotel, the name of which, by some bit of impure chance, had been scribbled on the face of the business card I had thrust into his hand.

"Mademoiselle DiMartino, she is eternally grateful," he told me, his tone somewhat guarded. His profession had taught him to be judicious when handling the issue of celebrity indebtedness.

I stared at him coldly. "If that's the way she feels," I said, "I would have thought she'd have the decency to tell me herself." My lack of empathy was not forced. I had anticipated gratitude expressed at the personal level. This second-hand dismissal would not do at all.

"I assure you, Mr. Waxout, the diva would have come if the doctors permitted. Unfortunately..." He shrugged.

"You say you are her manager?" I said. "What is she? Some little actress? A tap dancer?"

He was aghast. "Consuela DiMartino," he cried. "You have not heard of Consuela DiMartino? Prima Donna?"

"Oh, a girl singer. Everybody to his own way of making a buck, I guess."

"You do not understand, Mr. Waxout—"

"Take the doctors here at this hospital," I interrupted. "They're sure not going to die broke. Know what they're charging for this room? You wouldn't believe it. Thirty-six dollars a day. They'll play hell getting thirty-six bucks a day out of me. Here I go do some people a favor and what do I get out of it? A hospital bill."

Monsieur Brichant was not dull. That afternoon when I departed from my sterilized entombment I was informed that my bill had been paid by something identified as ConMar Enterprises, Consuela DiMartino president. Cure attained by application of that new medical drug: corporate write-off.

Thus Consuela had delivered me, as a gift, the ideal lever with which to pry my way into her swaddled private life—indignation. It chances to be a weapon that I have learned to wield with the best of them.

"How dare you, Madam," I screeched at her in her hotel apartment. "I am not a charity case awaiting the meddling of your cold-blooded munificence. I am quite able to finance the upkeep of my own body."

My assault had commenced as soon as Consuela's maid admitted me to the living room.

"Oh, Sir, I'm so sorry. It's just....we just assumed that we should pay the hospital bill. Your quick action at Whitman's possibly saved my career."

"How any intelligent person could be guilty of such indiscretion is beyond me." My words were still strong but the rancor was fading. "You do, I might add, give the appearance of intelligence. What are you, about 25 years old?" (The DiMartino was 29.)

"How can I answer that," she said smiling. She was regaining her footing in this more familiar repartee. "Let us say I am of an age where I no longer consider the topic suitable."

She tipped her chin up and drenched me with her famous laugh (Tosca doubting Mario.) "Is that how old I look to you, Mr.....ah, forgive me I'm terrible with names."

"It hardly surprises me, Madam. 'The little bald-headed man in the hospital, throw him a crumb. Pay his bill for him. No, no, don't bother me with his name'."

She threw up her hands and twirled away from me (Salome, I think.) "Ah, I have insulted you some more. How can I undo this?"

"You might start by ordering my hat."

"Oh, must you leave so soon?" She said and was not actress enough to keep the relief from her voice.

To answer your question, my dear: no.

"If you don't mind a bit of advice," I said, "you should start saving your money. Not throw it around in misguided charity. You are evidently doing rather well just now." I looked around at the room. "But girl singers are a dime a dozen. You can't expect to get by on your good looks much longer." Ha, but didn't that pinch. It even exploded my name to her memory.

"Are you for real, Mr. Waxout? Pierre told us about your, what will we call it: naiveté? Let me relieve your mercenary fears. Last year I toured the three civilized continents: here, South America, and of course the motherland of opera. My income for the year was exceeded in the field of entertainment by one person only, a bullfighter in Spain. I am not a baby-voiced little singer. I am not an object for financial pity. I am not to be lectured by a middle-aged American rabbit, or babbit, or whatever it is they call you commercial people."

"An opera singer?" I hissed. "You are an opera singer? Are you lying to me, Madam?"

"Lying?" she raged. "Does this sound like lying?"

She unleashed the DiMartino diaphragm. The stunning wave crest of an aria issued from the lovely mouth and ricocheted around the room. The window glass shrunk in its frame, the plaster hugged itself to the wall, and the nape of the rug smoothed itself in all directions away from the diva. And a door at the far end of the room burst open and two men flung into the room.

The man in the lead, the one with the white face, was Monsieur Pierre Brichant, Consuela's manager. Behind him came Mr. Scott Valboa, the poor chap who was well on his way to being replaced in Miss DiMartino's affections by my humble self.

"What in heaven's name are you doing?" M. Brichant screamed at the diva. "Have you lost sanity?"

"Honey, you shouldn't blast out like that," Mr. Valboa chided tenderly, attempting to reduce the excess in Brichant's criticism.

The DiMartino was not impressed. With Carmen's malevolent eye she explained my presence and the conversation that had evoked her rash performance. M. Brichant was of the opinion that I should be horsewhipped, and said so. His eye, though, held none of that sly cornering apprehension of a Groucho Marx and he of course did not add: If only I had a horse. Mr. Valboa suggested I leave.

"You can discontinue this witless charade," I said coldly. "this touching concern for her voice. Who do you think you're fooling? She could get on stage and sing through a bridle and bit and still get ten curtain calls."

"True, certainly. Because she is the DiMartino." Her manager snapped. "But the vocal chords are not for such abrupt abuse. With sufficient practice, then she can—"

"Bah, you choose to misunderstand me," I said. "If I'd known I was dealing with a pack of opera charlatans, I'd have left her poisoned in the restaurant."

I turned to leave. My sleeve grabbed by the diva's taloned claw. "Explain yourself," she demanded.

"Yes, Mister," Scott Valboa said evenly. Either you've been misinformed or you're going to get a punch in the jaw." It was not bravado for the lady, the lad sounded sincere. I would have to remember that he favored simple solutions.

"What is there to explain?" I said, removing the DiMartino's hand with untender force. "Those who deal in fraud, in gullibility, must recognize that they will occasionally encounter someone who is not gullible."

"We're talking about opera, buddy," Scott Valboa pointed out. "Not about fraud, or whatever the hell you're talking about."

"Come, come, we are adults, are we not?" I could not have been more condescending. "I believe we are all fully aware that opera is one of the most blatant frauds ever flung in the face of the putty-minded public. One of the oldest—and of course, most lucrative, frauds on record. You folks should really maintain your perspective, recognize that every person you meet will not be as stupid as your ticket buyers."

Their eyes were stunned. I added to their burden my slowly uncoiled smile of superiority.

"Bah, a madman," M. Brichant muttered in French and turned away.

Miss DiMartino looked at Scott Valboa, her pretty mouth pulled slightly open in disbelief. "This man, is he joking?" she asked Scott. Turning to me she said, "Do you mean you do not understand opera? You do not believe that there are those men and women, gifted by the Almighty, who can sing music as only a handful of those alive in the world can sing?"

"And who are capable of the years and years of hellish training required to discipline those voices to handle opera," Scott Valboa added, appending the proper self-sacrifice factor to the lady's generalization.

"I believe there are some freaks around, sure," I said, "lots of money can be made out of birth defects. Take P.T. Barnum."

Scott Valboa stepped toward me with his right hand in a fist. Consuela grabbed his arm and brought him to heel.

You're doing rather well, Augustus, you do indeed have their attention. But I would advise a redirecting of the heresy. Establish a less personal target for them, old man.

"An individual who is born with an unusual voice has a right to exploit it, I suppose," I conceded. "But when they misuse that...uh, talent, when they make a very soft living by deliberately perpetuating the myth of music they earn nothing from an intelligent man but contempt. To me a bank robber exhibits greater honesty."

"The 'myth of music'? What are you saying now?" Consuela demanded.

"Exactly what I say, Madam. The myth that there is an identifiable value to music per se. The delusion, I will admit, is centuries old. But what could be more absurd than the belief that a particular pattern of sounds, has within it more beauty, more emotion, or humility, or excitement than some other particular pattern of sounds?"

"Pierre is right, you <u>are</u> mad!" Valboa said, shaking his head as if to dislodge my words. Ah, but then the lad concocted a rebuttal.

"Tell me this, how the hell do you explain the reaction, the very visible reaction, you see in people when they hear one of your so called 'patterns of sound'? Haven't you ever seen a Frenchman cry while listening to the 'pattern' of the Marseillaise?"

"Certainly. And I have seen Mr. Pavlov's dogs salivate when they heard him ring their food bell. This *music* you speak of, it is another learned response. Play one of your crackpot symphonies or operas to an infant and watch his level of appreciation. He'll cry, most likely, because the noise hurts his ears. Bach, Beethoven, Brahms, the three 'B's"—the three blackguards is more like it. Growing rich on the conditioned reflexes of the peasants."

"You stupid man!" The diva scorned. "*YOU* are the absurdity. I have never heard such blasphemy!"

"What can you expect?" M. Brichant said wearily from the couch. "What can this nuts-and-bolts mechanic from Portland, Oregon know about opera?"

Ah, how astute of you, Mr. Manager. You have had the wit to investigate the Good Samaritan.

It was time to add a bit of depth to Mr. Clifford Waxout; get a few structural I-beams anchored behind the opinionated-ass false front they had seen thus far.

"It's funny that there are some of your fellow Europeans, eminent gentlemen, who will tell you the same thing I'm telling you," I said to Brichant in French. "I know one man who would laugh in your face if you told him there was any legitimacy to your 'world of opera'. And I believe Senor Picasso must be credited as being rather familiar with the ingredients of true art."

"I am not aware that Pablo Picasso has ever spoken out against opera." Brichant said. My use of his own language, even with the carefully applied edging of an American accent, had scratched away some of the protective cover on his contentment. Actually the three of them had become more alert. It had occurred to them that possibly there were no fools in the room.

(The real Clifford Waxout, I should mention, could, with just an average level of mumbling, at least order from a French menu.)

"For publication, perhaps not," I answered Brichant. "Why would he bother? Ask him in private conversation sometime, if you dare. I believe you will find my denouncement as a gentle breeze compared to Picasso's hurricane."

"He never gave me any criticism," Miss DiMartino said, genuinely puzzled. "You recall, Pierre, Pablo was at Contessa d'Monteynne's with us that night the wife of the French Premier, Madam de P______ was discovered in the greenhouse with that American newspaper correspondent, what was his name? He had that fascinating story about escaping from Hitler's fortress at Berchtesgaden disguised as Josef Stalin."

Well bless me, a mutual acquaintance!

"That sounds like Dean Noble," I said to Consuela. She nodded, her eyes startled. I chuckled and shook my head in wonder. "So old Dean took on Madam de P______ in the greenhouse? Can't say I blame him, she is a striking looking woman. The poor Premier."

Those of you who have turned the pages (lovingly it is hoped) of a journal of mine titled The Statue of Liberty Commission will know that the molesting of beautiful women was an act not in the least alien to Mr. Dean Noble. Commendably rapacious chap.

"But the point is, Mr. Waxout," Consuela pursued logic, "that Senor Picasso never said anything to me about not liking opera. He was most gallant, was he not, Pierre?"

"Of course not, Mademoiselle," I said, with simpering patience. "Pablo is of an age when one does not embarrass pretty women. He enjoys them. But have you ever seen his mural at the Le Doux villa outside Welborn, on the wall facing the gardens? There, ten feet tall and twenty feet in length, is Senor Picasso's judgment of your world of opera. There in brash color is his indictment against the fraud of opera and in particular the performers of same. Admittedly Pablo was a bit drunk. The squirting of the oils through the goatskin wine bag was not a successful innovation. But then the resulting obscurity in the detail does leave the identity of the central figure, the soprano with her conniving green eye, somewhat in doubt." I believe I have mentioned the lovely green of DiMartino's eyes.

"Actually, I guess we were both a bit drunk that night," I giggled.

"You are a personal friend of Senor Picasso?"

"I wouldn't say *friend*, Mademoiselle. The age differential is too severe. We have friends in common. Then Pablo is fond of some American writers whose works are hard to come by in French editions: Jack Erlich, Norb Fagan, Joe Gores. I am occasionally asked for a translation of the more Americanized passages. To tell the truth Pablo can be a bit of a bore with his night cables, some of them five pages long. But Ernie Hemingway keeps telling me I've got the con in that department."

"The *con*? You mean some sort of confidence game?"

"No, no, my dear," I explained. "The con is short for conning station. Naval term. The man with the con is the man in control on the bridge. Papa—" I turned to Scott Valboa, the other pupil in the group—"that's Mr. Hemingway's nickname."

"I know his god damn nickname," Scott replied. Almost invariably you will have a surly one or two in the classroom.

"Of course," I conceded. "Anyway, Papa is a great one for assigning responsibilities. When I raise some fuss about this assistance to Senor Picasso, Papa always levels a finger at me along the rim of his ever-present gin glass and says, 'That's the least you can do, you god damn plutocrat. That's you contribution to keeping that pure blade of Spanish steel properly polished." I always lose the argument," I concluded, with my helpless shrug.

"No!" Monsieur Brichant said. "I find it difficult—no I find it *impossible*—to believe Senor Picasso could be so misled, so wrong."

"Wrong, Monsieur? Is it Pablo and I who are so wrong? Or is it the trained dogs that pay you and Miss DiMartino good money to have their saliva glands actuated who are wrong?"

"Wait a minute," Scott Valboa charged into the conversation. "All we've got so far is some guy named Waxout saying Pablo Picasso doesn't like opera."

I turned on the young man my 'smile made of all sweet accord' (a terrible thing to see) and said, "My dear boy, how often have you seen Senor Picasso in a box at the Paris Opera? Or you, Mademoiselle?" I said glancing at Consuela.

"Well, never," the sweet diva admitted. "But he has lived in Spain so long, said he'd never enter France while the Nazis were in occupation. The Germans are now gone of course but evidently Senor Picasso has developed the Mediterranean habit. He does not come to Paris." Which may explain, my dear, why I selected Senor Picasso to illustrate my point.

"Even if he visited the city every weekend, my dear, I am certain you would not find him perched in a box at the Paris Opera inhaling that stageful of sham. As for myself, I am proud to state that I have never been milked of one thin dime by you, my dear, nor any of your frightful contemporaries."

"Ah! In other words, Mr. Waxout, you are condemning an art you have never even witnessed?" From Monsieur Brichant. It was not difficult to direct the Frenchman.

"Must one participate in a firing squad to appreciate the guest of honor's discomfort?" I asked, supercilious as ever.

"Why don't you come tonight and see how wrong you are?" Scott Valboa said. "Do you know anything about Aida?"

"Excellent, Scott," Brichant said to the young man. "Yes, Mr. Waxout, Mademoiselle DiMartino is performing Aida here in Washington. Will you pit your skepticism against the magic of Giuseppi Verdi?"

"Hmmm, tonight you say? The squash game with Senator Dempsey could be cancelled...How much are the tickets?"

"Pierre," the diva said before Mr. Brichant could rise to my bait, "I'm not certain I want such animosity staring back at me from the audience."

"Consuela..." Brichant said kindly, chiding the juvenile objection. "Very well, Mr. Waxout, the experiment will not cost you a franc. You will be a guest of the diva."

"Well, the price is right," I chuckled. "Besides it's a bit embarrassing beating Senator Dempsey too often. If he gets to be president he might try to get his money back by putting a special tax on air conditioners. That's my business, Waxout Industrial Air Conditioners."

"Yes, I know," Pierre said, writing a note on a business card.

"What do you mean, 'if Senator Dempsey gets to be President?'" Scott Valboa said. "There's not much doubt about it is there? They're certainly not going to nominate Old '76 again."

I shrugged. "You never know. Old '76 has one thing going for him, he's the President of the United States now. He beat the opposition once. 'Track record' is the term."

"As little as I know about your American politics, Mr. Waxout, I must agree with Scott," Brichant said. "There is little doubt in my country that your President '76 will not be nominated to run again. If you will present this card at the ticket office they will give you the choice seat in the house." I accepted the card and placed it in my note case. (You, dear reader, will be relieved to learn that my billfold had not been stolen from me in Whitman's Restaurant after all. Once I departed the establishment I discovered that my suspicions regarding the maitre d' had been foundless. The billfold was found wrapped to my ankle, of all places, secured to my shinbone by a rubber band.)

"The President may be a nut," Scott Valboa said as I picked up my hat. "All that '76 stuff: 76 push-ups every morning, 76 suits of clothes, 76 painted on his yacht, his airplane, everything he owns—"

"And 76 enemies out of every 100 men who give him their trust," Mr. Brichant commented.

"Yeah, but at least he does appreciate opera," Scott Valboa said. "The President of the United States doesn't share your view of opera, Mr. Waxout. In fact next month, on the 13th, Consuela is giving a recital at the White House. The President and his wife will be there."

"And of course, 76 guests," Mr. Brichant said. He glanced at Scott Valboa with parental patience and said to me, "I would appreciate it if you would keep the White House recital to yourself, Mr. Waxout. Such affairs are to be secret until announced by the President's staff, you understand?"

"Sure," I said. "Old '76's private life is an item of flagrant disinterest to the people I'll be seeing in Washington. It's what the ape does behind his desk in the Oval Office that worries us. Okay, I just might be able to squeeze in Aida tonight. I'll see."

"Even if you do not enjoy the singing," Miss DiMartino said with verve, "you will see Theresa Orlando's histrionics in the role of Amneris. I am told that she does a miraculous job of making you forget her weight, her age, and the fact that she does not sing."

"Consuela, Consuela," M. Brichant moaned, "let's not go into that again. She was the only mezzo available..."

I left them to their shallow preoccupations. And of course I attended the performance of Aida that evening. I would have done so even without the kind invitation, even had it required an expenditure of my own funds. There was need to rub the personality of Clifford Waxout rather thoroughly upon Miss DiMartino prior to the 13th of the next month. How kind of Mr. Valboa to mention the private concert for The President of the United States. The subject could now be reintroduced with total casualness by myself. Poor Mr. Brichant and his grave request that I maintain the secrecy of the concert date. Certainly I would not gossip about the affair. Had I not kept the same secret for the past two months? Was not this secret, in a sense, the very ballast restraining Mr. Clifford Waxout to the floor of the Pacific?

So that evening I watched Consuela DiMartino slug out Aida's tragic battle on the banks of the Nile. It was, as a matter of fact while I sat in M. Brichant's private box awaiting the curtain's rise that I heard of the curious incident that had occurred in the lives of the Bridgeport, Connecticut police.

Two ladies in an adjacent box were discussing the ripe affair.

Evidently, if one was to believe Washington's leading newspaper, The Post, the Bridgeport police had opened a locker at the main station of the New Haven Railroad and discovered therein the left leg and left arm of a woman.

"The police are quite puzzled," the lady with a white ermine cloak resting over the back of her chair said to her companion.

"You know that nice Chief Gallagher up there, George helped him get the job? Well, he said his department is proceeding on the assumption that these human...ah, remnants are the residue of some illegal violence."

"But why such a fuss?" the matron with the green velvet gown asked. "I'll admit the burial was ...well, unorthodox, but the Post had it on page one."

"Because the same thing happened in Louisville, Kentucky the other day," White Ermine explained. "A decapitated head tumbled from a locker in the bus station in Louisville, a young woman's. She had a key clenched in her teeth. The police used that key to open the locker in Bridgeport."

"Does the head from Louisville belong to the leg and arm from Bridgeport?"

"That's what the police don't know. They've brought in these experts, I suppose they mean some of those mortician people, to try and piece the thing together, determine the degree of cohesion in the investigation."

"Piece together," Green Velvet giggled, "Edna, that's terrible."

"And they're not making much progress," White Ermine (Edna) said. "You know men. They're fighting over jurisdiction. Is it a Kentucky case or a Connecticut case? The Post quoted a Captain Goldway of the Connecticut State Police who said, 'They may have the head there in Kentucky but we've got the arm. And it's the arm that's got fingerprints'. It's interesting, the value system that takes over once you die."

"Rather a cold-blooded attitude," Green Velvet commented. "But I guess that's the way policemen have to be."

Yes, my dear, unhappily your observation is valid.

"They are rather certain it's the work of the same fiend. They've found words written on all the parts. The head had the word 'steel' on the forehead. The leg had the word 'around'. And the arm had the word 'his.'"

"Steel, around, and his? What does it mean?"

"Nobody knows. The Connecticut police captain was rather amusing on the TV broadcast this afternoon. He said, 'We here in Connecticut are less than titillated by this affair.' And they've found another key."

"Another locker key?" Green Velvet said excitedly.

"Yes. It was tied on the big toe of the Bridgeport leg. They're trying to find the locker it fits now."

The house lights started to dim. I leaned toward the box of my informative neighbors and smiled. "Ah, wouldn't you concede, ladies, that the case of the scattered female limbs is mighty shy on whimsy?"

"I beg your pardon, Sir," White Ermine said stiffly. The darkness split us.

The Diva, to my ear, was in excellent form. I did however, hear a few negative comments in the lobby during intermission: "Yes, rather beautiful, of course, but you should have seen her Aida in Copenhagen. Superb." "Are you serious? Copenhagen? Why the ruddy bombers virtually destroyed Copenhagen's acoustics during the war. Now DiMartino in London last year, that was Aida!" Perhaps my estimate had been hasty.

While my expertise as an opera critic may be in question there is another area in which my judgment was apparently as acute as ever. I overheard this chap in the men's room giving concurrence to an intriguing conclusion that I had developed while watching DiMartino swirling about the stage, "I still say she's got the best looking ass of any dame in opera today, pound for pound, bar none." Here, here.

I left my box at the opera as the priests were joyfully lowering the stone slab over Aida and Radames in the temple of kindly old Vulcan. Back stage I loitered in the area of the star's dressing room until Miss DiMartino emerged from her premature burial. By Gadfry, but she resurrected in fine fettle.

Consuela was walking with her maid to whom she spoke in Italian. I stepped out, invading the area of their engrossed conversation. The diva was startled.

"Oh, I didn't expect you backstage," she said, "But I was very aware all during the performance that you were in the audience."

I was certain she had forgotten my name again. "There was no indication that you were absorbed with anything but the heroine's complex allegiances," I said, rather formally. "I must admit, Diva, that I was quite impressed with one item I did observe on the stage. It is an item that—"

As I spoke I let Consuela see my bold eye laid hold of Aida's greasepaint and proceed with an evaluation of the contours beneath the brown stain pavement.

"—I personally value very highly. Regardless of my basic opinions about music and opera there is a human relationship that emerges anytime you place people, men and women, in contact with each other. A relationship—"

The diva saw my eyes penetrate through the Ethiopian slave girl veneer and take a hot grip on the anatomical stress points of Consuela DiMartino.

"—that is woven from the ingredients Mother Nature plants in each of us. It is these ingredients, and they are volatile, occasionally flammable, ingredients that must be shaped and disciplined to our needs—"

The dawning appreciation Consuela saw as my eye continued its forage of her brief costume was not forced or synthetic; the diva, all112 pounds of her, was molded with the classic soundness of lapstreak.

"—and it is the disciplining of these human assets that I insist on at my factory, in the relationships developed by my employees;

male and female, day and night, week after week."

She blinked, bringing her mind back to focus. My last sentence had not tracked with some thought structure she was erecting. "You insist with the men and women at your factory...? You insist on what relationship?"

"Craftsmanship, my dear," I said. I took the diva's robe from the maid's arm and stepped behind Consuela, to adjust the garment over her shoulders. "People working together in a dedicated display of craftsmanship," I continued. "That's what impressed me about your production, a remarkably disciplined display of craftsmanship by every person involved, musicians, lighting, set design."

I patted the robe on her shoulders with both of my hands. "Best wear this. The theater must have a rather efficient air conditioning plant. Might even be a Waxout unit." (There you are my dear, a name to work with.) I moved around in front of her and took another rude swipe with my eye at the twin mounds where her breasts thrust boldly against her robe.

"There were a few other observations that overtook me during the play," I said sincerely as my eyes held hers. "They relate to you personally, oddly enough." I shook my head at the wonder of this. "I'd really like to explore them with you, if you are at all interested? Unfortunately just now I have to catch a train to New York."

"A performer is always interested in the opinions of others," she smiled. "Probably too interested. Ah, perhaps the next time you are in Washington, if you give me a call..." She was ready to dismiss me.

"There is one puzzling thing," I said, committing here my heavy field pieces. "That elderly lady who played the role of Amneris..."

"Madam Orlando," Consuela said tartly.

"Yes, Madam Orlando," I said with just the proper slyness to my smile. "Was it my imagination or did the stage actually list several degrees to port and starboard on her every entrance?"

The diva's laugh was a lovely sound. We agreed to a late dinner on my return to Washington the following evening.

Now, there has been much published over the centuries on the plight of the Beautiful Woman; on the attrition imposed on her by the less endowed. For example, she is haunted by the axioms we have developed to prequotient her intelligence: beautiful but dumb, comes to mind; pretty face, empty head. We have even provided m'lady with a very precise gage with which she may measure her allure, skin deep. Rather a frail stretch of armor, wouldn't you say?

We drive her, the Beautiful Woman, to loneliness, for we advise her to be ever suspicious of the friendship offered by her plainer sisters. And she is, of course, lastingly the target for bestiality from males, plain and otherwise.

We keep her ever conscious of the withering inroads of the years. Our jackal are constantly circling the dear, waiting to herald the wrinkle, the gray, the sag.

Actually we are never really at ease until we have put her into the ground.

Still, with all, who will say that the price is not right?

One burden shackled about the slender neck of the Beautiful Woman, one that she in no way deserves, is that imposed by the boor. These are the men she encounters in the process of normal day-to-day living who are apparently out to avenge some bitter self-estimates. They find absolution, a strange comfort, by clawing gaping wounds in the proud beauty. Their flag is instant defiance and their weapon is churlishness. Among the members of this surly brigade: The snappish young man at the ticket counter. The calculatingly sloppy deliveryman who slams down his wares. The brusque traffic cop with his belligerent glare. The moribund public servant, a customs official say, across the desk or counter with his lifeless expression and list of negative regulations.

But then, there is wisdom to be harvested here, my friend. It is also by use of this defiance, this disinterest, that you will find quick access to my lady's attention. If you can tip her self-confidence off center for a moment, expose for a second the soft underbelly of her serenity, you can surrey inside her wall of awareness. By the time she rocks back to center you will, if you have been alert, if you have been properly about your business, you will have penetrated several layers of her emotional defenses. You will, at this point, assume the label of 'acquaintance'.

Should you aspire to the next plateau, you will again tip the lady off center and squeeze a bit deeper into her emotional labyrinth. Around a corner, down a passageway, across an open court, and there it is: the hall reserved for the lady's friends. You enter.

It is a process of human relations as old as man. In a given period of time on a given number of encounters two persons will invariably respond to the basic ground rules. It's as natural as Man's bent for manufacturing from the sparest of ingredients thorough-going discontent.

Over a several year period Consuela DiMartino and I would have certainly become warm friends. Recall though, I had less than two weeks. In that period I had to take up residence not only in the Hall of Friends, but also in the boudoir beyond.

Thus the natural had to be discarded. Load up with grapeshot, Colonel; we're going to smash our way through that ruddy line. You'll find it filed under 'G', Colonel, as in Guile.

Here we go, my sweet Consuela.

For our initial dinner, on the evening following Aida, it was important that I spin a proper operating web for Clifford Waxout, one that contained no distracting irritants such as: poverty, parochialism, lack of influence. I chose as a site therefore the dining room of the Metropolitan Club. We achieved entrance to the somewhat exclusive club with a membership card still damp from my superb penmanship. While approaching our table I whispered to my lovely date, "There's the Vice President. When he waves please do not encourage him. The Party insists that I write his speeches, but I'll be damned if I'll dine with him."

Next the Club's dining room staff. "The lady will have the cannelloni," I told the white-haired Negro waiter. "As for myself... now let me see." I closed the huge brocade-covered menu and stared over the waiter's shoulder with a look of global perspective. "It's spring here in the Northern Hemisphere. Middle of autumn in Cape Town, of course," I mused. Then the full impact dawned on me. "And in Argentina!" I cried delightedly at the startled waiter. "The Pampas, lush with burned out clover. You do have Argentine beef of course?" I asked.

The waiter said he thought they had. "Fine. Now, you take a quarter pound of lean Argentine beef. You chop it into an even consistency and form it into a patty. Fry, over a natural gas flame for eleven seconds per side. Turn only once," I cautioned sternly. "Place on a soft roll; not French bread. One slice of partially green tomato on the meat. A folded leaf of California lettuce. One half a tablespoon of ketchup—I don't want any guff from the Head Chef; go out and purchase the ketchup if none is on hand—and place just under the top bun a slice of Bermuda onion, one sliced within the past 12 hours. That should do it."

"Yes, sir," said the waiter. "Anything to drink with dinner?" he asked, his eyes cautiously on my face.

"Hmmm. Yes, a bottle of Mexican beer; Poncho's Cellar if you have it. Otherwise any brand from a distillery located south of Ensenada."

As the waiter withdrew, Consuela said puzzled, "Clifford, that concoction you ordered, do you know what it sounded like? One of those dreadful hamburgers the Americans are always eating in their backyards."

"Of course, my dear," I smiled. "I've been dying for one all day. I was but attempting to spare the man the embarrassment of writing 'hamburger, with the trimmings' on his pad. He'd have been the laughing stock of the kitchen."

As it turned out the Master Chef accompanied my order to our table. He stood very straight and said, "Herr Customer, this is how you have ordered this thing?"

I looked under the top bun, punched the meat patty with my fork, and nodded approvingly. "Well done," I said.

"Nein," the Master Chef snapped. "Medium rare." Suddenly he giggled. "In mine twelve years in this United States," he said shaking his head, "I am never to get the chance to..." He turned away waving to me saying, "Enjoy, enjoy."

The incident amused Consuela as indeed it had been designed to. She was a delightfully civilized woman. "Clifford, do you often do things like that? Where do you find the opportunity in a place like Portland, Oregon?"

I'm sorry, my dear, but I cannot permit you to isolate the short period I have access to you to trivial chit-chat.

"Pardon me, my dear, would you mind changing seats with me?"

"Uh?...Oh, of course not."

We carried out the complex exchange, my still-nervous waiter assisting with repositioning the dishes. Within a few minutes Consuela found me more distracted, staring off frequently at something behind her. When she finally brought herself to look around the edge of her high-backed chair she found that my interest was in the bare shoulders and ample cleavage of a blond-haired lady two tables away. The blond was several years Consuela's senior.

This indeed, my friend, was the vexing portion of the...ah, I suppose "seduction" is still the best word. I was attempting to station the diva and myself in a classic romantic relationship; the hunter and the hunted. Consuela had been assigned the role of the hunter. The task was to get her properly on track, get her motivated for the kill. The bait, the personality of Clifford Waxout, had to be served up in a rather complex package. There had to be a sensuousness to the man, a bit of mystery, a tricky degree of remoteness, tenderness, and of course, and probably most important, that subtle air of silent pain, delicate sorrow.

To an engagement of this sort you do bring your own collection of tools, but your major weapon is the emotional composition, the ticking brain cells, of the second party. The lady seated across from me at the Metropolitan Club for instance was abnormally vulnerable in a certain area. My battle plan thus involved that basic deployment of forces: the two pronged attack on the flanks. Martial simplicity, old man.

On the one flank we would manipulate her weakness. At the same time there would be presented to the other flank overt evidence to the lady that Clifford Waxout saw her not as a female prize of international proportions but rather just another pretty face in the crowd. (Ah, Consuela, you must forgive me. There was just so little time.)

Thus the plan, now the execution.

The lady's blind spot, the weakness I spoke of, as you may have guessed, was Miss DiMartino's complete submersion in the world of Opera. It is a world similar to that of the theater of politics where a single, breathing human, rather than a product or a service, is the focal point for massive concern. Now, when you enter the market place with an extremely perishable commodity, rather than a sturdy mechanical devise or some plastic-wrapped chemicals, you must reduce the perishability, the fragility of your offering. Once you have your human, money-making curio in hand—say you are the manager of the dog-and-pony show; Monsieur Brichant in the case of point—one of the least desirable environments for your prize is the one we call: a normal life. My God, the incident of contracting common colds from germ spraying shopkeepers and grubby bus passengers is sufficient to dictate a program of benevolent, but firm, isolation for your top-of-the-line.

The DiMartino and her world of Opera: She awakes each morning with one slim hand at her throat. Is it still there? Next, the lubricating from the precious vocal chords any foreign contaminant that may have lodged there during the night. Then the exercising of the voice box to ensure that it has not lost its memory.

Meanwhile the diva, those of Miss DiMartino's eminence, is exposed only to other individuals who, by profession or livelihood, are as interested in Madam's commercial survival as she.

They are not likely to bring her any intelligence from the world at large other than those of mutual interest: the announcement of that season's program at LaScala; a priority item. The Metropolitan's new fiscal policy; her business manager's passion. The tepid reaction from the audience to a performance by some hated rival; good meaty juice on a cold afternoon.

Then our heroine's private life away from opera is rather a circular tour of familiar ground. On a weekend visit: The Riviera, Cape Cod, Big Sur, her host is not likely to overlook neither her eminence nor her specialty. He will surround her with handpicked guests who are certainly not there to instruct her on their own interests and life styles. They will instead use the opportunity to catalog their own contacts, experience, and infatuation with her world.

Insular, insular, thy name is opera.

What then do you serve up to such a lady? What might quicken her pulse? Touch at her timid lust? Well, now, how about this interesting chap, Clifford Waxout? Admittedly a bit on the efficient side, and he really should do something about that balding dome. But then, there is a refreshing air about him, what with his disquieting roving eye and his aura of accomplishment in the worlds of government, art, and business.

And, beneath the frontal wall of efficiency and surefootedness, isn't there a peek now and then, perhaps just a whisper, of silent agony; a whiff of long buried tragedy? Must he carry it forever by himself? Is there no creamy shoulder for his bowed head, no breast where his hot tears may run?

At the Metropolitan Club I early commandeered the conversation and led it with precision into those areas that permitted me to become infuriatingly condescending as we unwrapped sentence-by-sentence Consuela's frail knowledge of the world marching along outside the opera walls. By the time the coffee arrived the poor thing was apologizing in every other sentence.

"You must think me an awful idiot, Clifford, but who is Raymond Bosworth again? I'm afraid I have him confused with the Governor of Kansas."

"No, no, Bosworth was the Secretary of the Navy in this country, the man who claimed the twelve destroyers had been leased to the Kansas Naval Reserve Unit. Once Peggy Crotteau, the French underground agent, stole the complete file from Bosworth's attaché case while he was still sleeping in the New Orleans motel and turned it over to my committee, we knew the destroyers were headed for Venezuela for half their true value. Now the French shipyards will get the contract from Venezuela, thanks to the work of your Monsieur Giral."

"That is the incredible part," sayeth the lady. "I have known Senor Giral for years as a director of the Paris Opera. To hear that he is an industrial spy, or secret agent, or whatever you call them—a manipulator of the policies of foreign governments is so...incongruous."

"He's been an operative in the field since before World War II," I said, with a nice professional snap. "Good man. Cleared everything through channels. Always had his microfilm properly developed. My information is Giral will retire shortly from M-5-Zero and will be awarded a medal by the French government. The whole story will come out then; less the classified stuff, of course."

"And Sir Thomas Beecham is actually Senor Giral's English contact? How utterly amazing."

"That was the form during World War II. The Germans never suspected the message traffic that went out with each opera broadcast. Pickup locations, parachute drops, submarine landings, you know...the whole ruddy baggage. Sir Thomas and Giral made a great team."

"But I had no thought that these men were involved in anything but their careers. It..it makes one realize that one is leading a very sheltered life. Very sheltered indeed. Too damn sheltered."

I chuckled and reached to put a hand over hers. "Don't let the romantic aspect of it mislead you, my sweet. There's a lot of dirty-alley stuff too. Incidents you'd like to forget. A girl from Barcelona who traded loyalty and, yes, it was love, for a Nazi chateau with silk sheets..." The pain of that memory was of an intensity that momentarily strangled my voice.

"And believe me, Miss DiMartino, we are none of us immune from pure fear. There is a very special apprehension about awaking on the Orient Express at dawn slowing for a border-check with a false passport in your kit in which you know some hack in the Istanbul office has misspelled your name. Or riding a sled with a broken runner behind a team of played-out dogs in Kenya with a swarm of Mau Mau running up your back and losing your boot with the maps in the sole and feeling the drag on your forward speed as the ice solidifies around your ankle..."

"Kenya? Isn't that in Africa? I mean rather tropical and all for sleds?"

Ah, so your credulity does have a bottom, my dear.

"Not at all uncommon at the15,000 foot level of Kilimanjaro, young lady. It's about the only route still open to British Intelligence to get reports out of bloody Tanganyika, provided you can get past the damn Urundi and their blow guns." I let my eye wander away. The blond with the over-exposed bosom was preparing to leave. She bent forward delightfully to rise up from the chair that was pulled back for her.

Consuela took note of my lapse and started stirring her cold coffee. As her escort turned away to have a word with the maitre d', the blond turned and stared back toward me with a slight smile for a long second. She had not been unaware of my surveillance during dinner and had somehow misinterpreted my interest. One of the hazards of the game.

"You were saying that I should not be too quick to throw off my prosaic life, Mr. Waxout?" Ah, one loses ground when one does not pay sufficient attention to the timing. We were back to "Mr.

Waxout." Ladies, bless them, are really the masters of vengeance.

"I was only cautioning that there are bad times," I said, leaning my elbows on the table, bringing full attention back to home base. "But as in everything, there are memories; incidents I'd never sacrifice. God, will I ever forget the day we tried to teach Toscanini skin diving? There was Gabriel Miro, Bernard Shaw, and myself, and Pius, you know, the Pope. Well we were all spending a week on the gulf of Taranto..."

Admittedly, in the process of squeezing Consuela's circle of awareness of its minimum diameter it was necessary to super-impose a contrasting circle—the events of my life—the square footage which may have been somewhat multiplied by my exuberance. Then again, I had provided the lady an accurate account of those activities that have engrossed me since puberty; I suspect her degree of fascination would have been parallel. Her conclusions and her empathy toward me would I suppose have differed, but permit me this pedantry...she would have been fascinated. Judge for yourself, dear reader.

Successful progress is frequently measured by miniature signals. Consuela had appeared to enjoy the evening of Washington nightlife on the arm of the debonair Clifford Waxout. But ladies learn very early in the business of courtship to paint on an exterior cover of gaiety regardless of the reservations hidden behind the façade. It is possible they are born with this skill. Thus I had no trusted gage to go by until I delivered the maid back to her hotel and we tiptoed into the sensitive period of Farewell.

"Will...ah...will you be in Washington for long, Clifford?" Consuela asked me as we waited for her elevator.

I believe, sir, that your itinerary is being probed. Promising.

"How long is your Aida scheduled?"

"Another two weeks, until the 12th."

"Oh, is that why the White House recital is scheduled for the 13th?"

"No, no," she smiled. "One does not schedule the President of the United States to fit one's own agenda. The White House gave us their date. Pierre then arranged the Aida engagement."

"My business in Washington is completed for a while," I said as we entered the elevator. There were only the two of us in the car. I said nothing as the near-silent mechanism drew us upward. Once the flame has been applied, my son, one must allow it a period for draft. It is a refinement too often ignored by the untrained seducer.

As we emerged on the carpeted level of the 10th floor, I chuckled and said, "It has just occurred to me that I never did get around to telling you about my impressions as I watched your performance last night. Also there were a few comments in the lobby that you may find interesting."

"Oh, Clifford, I'd love to hear them."

"Good. At least you are not a coward."

She gave me her key and I unlocked the door to her apartment. I took her hand and kissed it softly. (She had had the foresight to remove her glove.)

"Now, I'll have to stand here and watch you go in," I said with a slight edge of humor. "There was an intriguing remark passed in the lobby last night. I want to know if the chap knew what he was talking about."

"I don't understand," she said lightly puzzled. "Had it to do with my entrances and exits?"

"Only your exits, my dear. This gentleman declared with considerable authority that Miss DiMartino possesses the cutest derriere in opera today. 'Pound for pound, bar none', was the way he put it."

"Mr. Waxout! That is absolutely obscene," she laughed.

I bent down and kissed her on the cheek. "May I call you next week?" I said, my eyes bluntly on hers. "I really should come back to Washington, if only to complete Senator Dempsey's squash lessons."

"Of course, Clifford, I'll be free every night except Wednesday.

That's when we have rehearsal for the White House affair." I don't know which blurred my senses more, the bottomless green eyes or the maid's honesty. (Speaking of honesty, Augustus, there was also the view of the lady's chest complex as you assisted her from the taxi. Does not that sight continue to roam your senses?) Her refreshingly forthright resume of her availability certainly provided adequate flexibility for a schedule.

I shook my head, obviously attempting to dislodge some magic from my brow. "I am beginning to believe you are an evil temptress, Madam," I murmured. "I'll call you Monday."

But she could not forget that she was, after all, the Female. As she said, "Good night, Clifford," there was just a glint of sure triumph in her eye. Thus, before she had closed the door fully I said, "Oh, Consuela..."

She paused and said, "Yes?"

"Would it be possible for Monsieur Brichant to join us? I'm certain he will be interested in the observations of the Oregon farm boy also." The luster faded from her eye on a wounded wing. Augustus, the most charitable assessment of your behavior is, I fear, heartless.

The following day I drove to Baltimore and made my three duty calls to Portland, Oregon. The call to wife Nell was concluded in 80 seconds. "Yes, I had the flat fixed," she responded. "Damn right," I barked. "How was Winnie's Best Seller Party? Never mind, I'll see you in a couple of weeks." Click.

My production manager, Fred Hoffman held me on the line for ten minutes providing me an insecure briefing on the decisions he had made at the Waxout Air Conditioning factory since my departure.

"Fine, fine," I said, as the statistics continued to numb my ear. "Just don't move too fast. Listen, Fred, there's something I forgot to tell you before I left. I put you in for a raise, $5,000.00. I left the memo for Accounting there in the office someplace. Or maybe down in Engineering someplace. You go ahead and put it through." That should keep old Fred busy.

The final telephone call went to *America's Americans,* Northwest Division, to the Secretary of the same, Polly Culver. For the first several sentences there was taut embarrassment at dear Polly's end of the connection. She did not release her tension until I interrupted her recital of the speaking engagements she had scheduled for me to ask her if she owned a black garter belt.

"Oh, Cliff, you're awful," she gushed. "My God, every time I think of it...right here in the office! Incidentally, Gloria quit on us. I'm not positive but I think that little snip was peeking. Oh, we were awful," she said giggling.

While we were going through our farewell I said, "And don't be surprised if you see my name in all the newspapers. I've thought of a great idea for getting *America's Americans* the kind of publicity we need. I can't tell you about it yet. You'll read about it."

"I...I can hardly wait," she said, dismally. "Cliff, you haven't been talking to those people in Middle Atlantic Division, have you? You haven't talked to Martin Crossfox? You know that that man is insanely jealous of your position in *America's Americans.* You haven't let him involve you in anything stupi...unorthodox?"

"Dear, Polly, I have talked to Mid Atlantic but this idea I have, it's my own idea. You'll see."

"I'm sure it will be marvelous, Cliff, if you thought it up." Again, the utter lack of confidence in the Director.

My dear, Polly, it's a pip!

Back in Washington the following week I descended upon Consuela DiMartino like an avalanche. Time was escaping in great 24-hour chunks. There were barricades to be leveled. First, the obstruction named Scott Valboa.

Scott was one of those fortunate chaps who had been forced to dig a glittering career out of a poverty-stained childhood in La Crosse, Wisconsin, U.S.A. He had been provided in this task the minimal assistance, his own two hands. Scott had foregone the enervating preoccupation of his high school schoolmates: the basketball, the drugstore lounging, the gasoline-fumed mating in the back seats of autos. Instead he secured for himself a few of those fragile gold keys tossed into circulation by disturbed men of wealth, college scholarships.

Scott buttressed the charity of the scholarships with the sweat from his body; waiter, cook, bottle-washer, a stern, monastic, joyless regimen. He emerged from the university campus six years later; a blond-headed, hard blue-eyed lead pipe, looking for heads to smash; a polished lead pipe, to be sure.

Another soul-less four years of apprenticeship slithered by before Scott arrived at an appreciable first goal—head publicist for the Cleveland Symphonic. In this capacity, a few years later, he met Consuela DiMartino. He was added to her retinue.

"But that sort of growing up, it takes something out of a man," Monsieur Brichant told me. Pierre was providing the Valboa biography. "A boy who lives too long on the edge of disaster, for the rest of his life there must be this very real insecurity. He will postpone decisions. He will hesitate rather than act. He will, I have observed, hold what he has, the embrace and the kiss of a famous woman, let us say. More than the kiss he will not try for. Another man, one who trusts his capabilities, he would carry the relationship forward, to the boudoir. Scott, he will not tamper with the existing structure. Bah! Youth!" He scattered several shrimp shells from his plate with his fork.

"In such a deadlock, what would one expect?" Pierre continued. "The woman to become the aggressor, to lead. And what does one find? The troubled observer, what does he find? Farce heaped upon farce. The woman cannot act. She is sealed. Twenty nine years of age—lusted after by a dozen satyrs on three continents—and still untouched!" He drank a long gulp of his wine. When he spoke again, his shoulders had hunched farther.

"I have watched her like a father since she was 17. I know. My God, I have led her into the snares of men whose reputations in such matters are international. Incompetent hulks of vanity! They returned me the same tortured, frustrated woman. The same hungry girl with her self-doubts, her grinding worries about the inability of her body to cooperate with her senses. Bah..." He paused and stared at his wine.

"I suppose it affects her work?" I asked quietly.

"Mr. Waxout," Pierre said, pointing his lobster pick at me, "even with your limited knowledge of the world of opera, surely you know of Carmen? The fiery Spanish gypsy, the earthy bohemian? Would not Consuela make a good Carmen?" He did not wait for an answer.

"Of course she would!" he exploded. "The greatest Carmen ever seen. Her presence, her body, she would be the Carmen they would never forget. To this day, to this day, she cannot bring herself to even learn the score!" He threw the pick into the empty lobster carcass on his plate.

"Does it affect her work? Mon Dieu! Of course. Why else would I connive against her virtue? You should have seen her five years ago when it was very bad. On stage she was a seductress like a store dummy, a Salome from a convent." A waiter summoned the gumption to remove our plates. Ours was the last table occupied in the restaurant. The waiter looked at our bottle of wine but I lifted it and replenished Monsieur Brichant's glass. Our servant slunk off into the gloom, toward the empty bar for another snifter of patience.

"I am glad to meet you, Mr. Waxout," Pierre said, the blur of drunkenness overtaking his voice swiftly now. "Yes, Mr. Waxout this past week I have watched, watched the care she takes—her gowns, her hair—when you are coming. I welcome you, Mr. Waxout. Not only because of these little dinners we have had, you and I. I do not meet many men in whose company I will permit myself to drink like this. Your way with the wine list, it is masterful, my friend, believe me. Ahhh, what is it? What is it? Promise, I think. You show promise, Mr. Waxout. I have rarely seen her so reluctant to leave the table, to get her sleep. Like tonight. It is encouraging after so long. But Valboa, he will not give her up easily. Timid to move ahead, as I said. But he is tenacious about what he already holds. And Consuela, unfortunately, she is as loyal as a lioness to those that need her..." He slapped the tabletop sharply with his palms.

"Ah, too much talk," Pierre said glancing around at the darkened room. "Too much grape. Good night, Mr. Waxout. Good night, my friend."

Good night. Good night, mon Pere. Thank you for your blessing.

Securing the decampment of Scott Valboa was not particularly laborious. He was young. His mental skein, once one peeled back the surface tissue, proved cavernous; a void containing a few luminous bats hanging upside down here and there.

There were, for instance, the lad's attempts to dominate the conversation at lunch (served in the rooftop restaurant of Consuela's hotel overlooking the Potomac River and the lush state of Virginia just beyond; no more lunches at Whitman's.)

"Well, they've found another locker," Scott announced as we seated ourselves around the table reserved daily for the DiMartino's lunch. "I mean the police."

"Another locker, Scott?" I said, encouraging the lad. He was about to blunder into a subject that would endear him to no one, particularly Consuela.

"You remember," Scott said eagerly, "the girl they've been finding in the lockers. Her head in a bus station locker in Louisville, Kentucky. A leg and an arm in a railroad station locker in Bridgeport, Connecticut. Last night they found the other arm and leg in a bus station locker in Lancaster, Pennsylvania."

"The story is here in the Washington Post," Monsieur Brichant commented, lifting the newspaper he had dropped next to his chair. "A much more interesting article appears on page—"

"Let me have that a minute, Pierre," Scott said holding his hand out for the newspaper. Pierre passed it to him. "The FBI is in on it now," Scott said as he thumbed to a particular inner page. "J. Edgar

Hoover and his boys don't fool around. Here's the rest of the story." He folded the paper and perused the write-up with intensity.

Consuela was attempting to catch my eye and Pierre's. I maintained a steady, attentive posture toward Scott, waiting to hear his bright, witty commentary regarding the juvenile absorption by the general public with the case of the wanderlust limbs.

"They've settled that stupid 'jurisdiction' business," Scott advised us without looking up from his reading. "All the parts: the head from Louisville, the arm and leg from Bridgeport, and this last arm and leg from Lancaster, are being flown to FBI Headquarters. That's more like it."

"I suppose a general housekeeping effort is in order," I said, my jocular tone attempting to set the stage for Scott's bitingly humorous commentary.

"Sure they have gathered the parts together," Scott assured me. "Otherwise nobody gets anyplace. Now the Bureau guys can take over from the hicks. Here's the significant bit here," He consulted a paragraph of newsprint. "The Head Agent in Philadelphia, K.O. Wilson, told the reporters: 'This office has been directed to assume command of the investigation. There is ample evidence, we feel, to presume a criminal infraction here of interstate proportions'. Well, hell yes," Scott agreed with the FBI. "The key found in one locker opened the next locker, didn't it? And all the pieces they've found so far have the same lettering on them. This arm from the Lancaster locker has the word 'neck' on it."

"Have any of the police agencies explored the possibility that they are dealing with the supernatural here?" I asked. "Perhaps the restless young woman is communicating from beyond the grave? I am, presuming of course, that the authorities have determined that she is deceased." My accompanying chuckle tapered off as I watched Scott Valboa's face retain its solemnity.

Now I glanced about for assistance. To Pierre first, then to Consuela. My expression said loudly, 'Is this young man serious?'" The Frenchman and the diva both let their eyes slip from mine, slightly ashamed that I should have stumbled upon a family secret.

"At least the police know the correct sequence for the words now," Scott babbled on. "The leg from Lancaster has the four words, 'Steel Around His Neck'. Whatever that means."

Consuela stirred. "What...? 'Steel Around His Neck'?" She looked at Brichant. "Why does that sound familiar, Pierre?"

"It does not to me, Diva," he shrugged. "From the lyrics of some opera, perhaps."

"The FBI thinks it might have some religious roots," Scott reported. "You know, some religious maniac taking on the role of the avenging angel. They've commissioned three Biblical scholars to, quote, 'Investigate a possible Old Testament connotation in the words Steel Around His Neck', unquote."

"And what have the legitimate religious maniacs discovered?" Brichant asked dryly.

"Pierre," Consuela chided her manager lightly.

"They have found one reference that might be relevant," Scott read on. "Yoked From Neck To Neck appears in the Bible."

"I would venture that they are on the wrong track there," I commented. "The victim is evidently a young woman, probably American. The quote from the Bible sounds like a reference to beasts of burden."

"Definitely incongruous," Brichant agreed with me and we smiled at each other. Consuela glanced at both of us, measured the camaraderie, and, almost visibly, relaxed against the back of her chair, contented.

"There's a gang of agents out now looking for the next locker," Scott pressed on. "There was another key with the Lancaster leg, tied to the big toe. A Lancaster official told the Post, quote, 'There's a good size chunk of this body unaccounted for yet.' Christ, that's pretty suave." Scott editorialized.

He refolded the newspaper neatly to the front page, "It's pretty obvious that we haven't seen the end of this thing," he said tasting the thought.

"One can almost feel America moving up to the edge of its chair," Consuela remarked. "Please, let's find something pleasant to talk about. What a glorious day."

Naturally I did not overlook Mr. Valboa's preoccupation with the case of the peripatetic limbs, and Consuela's lack of empathy for same. Each time Scott and I met in the diva's presence I provided the lad with the occasion to display his deductive cape-work. "Scott, good to see you again. The diva said she'd be out in a moment. Ah, here she comes. Hey, Scott, you're up on this young-woman-in-the-bus-station-locker-business. Did I read where the FBI has concluded the poor thing committed suicide?"

"Suicide?" sayeth the lamb. "My God, no. Don't you know the details? They found the head in..." and so on.

Or, 'Good evening, Scott. Well I'm certain you must be as relieved as the FBI to be rid of the locker rummaging?"

"Relieved?"

"Why..er, somebody told me it was all over. They've discovered the whole thing was a hoax. Advertising for some new line of luggage, or the like."

"But how could it be a hoax? The parts they've found are human parts. Flesh and blood..."

"Ah, good evening, Consuela. Has anyone ever mentioned your impeccable taste in eveningwear, young lady? Yes, go on, Scott. You were saying it couldn't be a hoax?"

"Where would they get a young girl's body? I mean those severed legs and arms came from some woman. Personally I think..."

It is frequently necessary in this life for the more able to assist the less fortunate. If Scott Valboa were ever to mount his immature preoccupation on the proper size canvas for m'lady's inspection there had to guidance and encouragement from a patron. Simple Christian charity, old man.

But the patron's duties are multiple. He must consider also the needs of the audience when the artist (Scott) becomes too immersed in the detail of his craft.

Scott (eagerly), "So, obviously somebody is cramming those blood-soaked parts of the girl in those lockers. The sooner the FBI starts looking beyond the obvious motives and concentrates on—"

"Scott, Scott, I think we've had enough about that unfortunate girl," speaketh the judicious patron (myself.) "Did anyone perchance hear the outcome of the Giant's game with the second-place team? That new manager, Dutch Barksdale, really has people believing he can beat the Giants."

"I certainly hope not," Consuela said laughing nervously, totally relieved that I had changed the subject. "ConMar Enterprises owns some baseball stock, including an interest in the New York Giants." (Yes, my young San Francisco readers, that's where your baseball heroes came from, New York.)

(Remind me, too, that I must pen an account of my own adventures in the world of United States' baseball. I 'batted', as they say, against the New York Giants once in a cozy enclosure called the Polo Grounds. Hopefully the remains of said structure will someday be excavated from beneath the existing 18-story apartment houses by dedicated archeologists who will surely stand back and cry in baffled voices, 'Now, what in God's name did 20th Century Man do in this strange place? Feed Christians to lions?' No, no, old man, occasionally Giants to Tigers; more frequently however Giants to a rather ferocious breed called a Dodger. Anyway, I must get it all on paper someday. Augustus Mandrell versus the New York Giants. Or, a more appropriate title, The Baseball Commission.)

I will admit that I, too, was not that fascinated by Scott Valboa's incessant reporting of the Lady in the Locker adventure. I have, by trade suffered a somewhat higher than average encounter with human violence but I have never really been at ease with, nor partial to, the Jack the Ripper school.

Disqualifying Scott intellectually was a relatively simple task. Getting Consuela to disown him was an entirely different matter. Pierre Brichant's estimate had been painfully accurate, the lady was absurdly loyal. The bumbling Valboa, sensing that this Clifford Waxout person was circling his campfire, clung to the diva, and she permitted the parasite to remain with his hollow fang at her throat.

The young man, for instance, insisted on being included in all of our Washington nightlife soirees. Consuela could not bring herself to deny him even though M. Brichant and myself, occasionally working in tandem, let it be known that the lad bored us relentlessly. ("Oh, Scott is coming with us?" with just the proper touch of disappointment.) This pose of stoic endurance on the part of the manager and myself was not in the least counterfeit. With regard to an evening where the revelers generate for themselves a small world full of charming gaiety I cannot say that Scott did not contribute. In all fairness to the young man I must disclose that he dressed beautifully.

All right, lad, you refuse to go quietly. I am forced then to pull the pins from the hand grenades.

Up until this point in time, about a week following my intrusion into the lives in the DiMartino entourage, Scott was gripped only with the uncomfortable sense that times had been more serene prior to the arrival of Clifford Waxout. During the second week there was a change. With increasing regularity Mr. Valboa observed the stranger from Portland, Oregon smiling warmly and suggestively to Consuela. What does it mean, lad, that secretive wink? What have those two been up to? This morning did the lady look as though she had not enjoyed a full night's sleep? Eh?

My awkward displays of intimacy were timed just so. Scott saw them, Consuela did not. The engrossing messages were delivered when the diva's eyes were not on my face. But Scott, whom I had maneuvered to a position just off Consuela's stern ("Would you be good enough to ask the hostess if I've had any message from Senator Dempsey, Scott? I'll get the table.") he witnessed my warm indiscretions and of course had to assume that I was receiving a sympathetic hearing from the lady.

The poor lad's mettle was not up to this level of abuse. He determined that he must fight and drew from his scabbard that bitter-steel sword of the weak and disorganized—jealousy. Happily he proved to be exceptionally talented in the proper flailing about with this unsavory weapon. Madam quickly found herself dreadfully fatigued by the lad. A woman may accept a man's sniveling, the self destruction of his pride in front of her (many of the dear things will even demand this) but the bombast, the threats inherent in undisciplined jealous outrage only a dull woman will enfold in her patience.

Three days prior to the recital for the President of the United States poor Scott blundered into a blind-alley ultimatum.

"I am not going to put up with that blowhard Clifford Waxout one more evening," Scott raged at Consuela, in front of the twinkling eye of Monsieur Brichant. "Either you go out with that insufferable hardware merchant, Consuela, or you go out with me."

"I've never heard such rubbish," replied the lovely diva. "What has happened to you lately, Scott? This evening I am dining with Pierre and Mr. Waxout. You may join or not, as you wish. I'm ready, Pierre."

As Consuela and Pierre exited the shabby encounter, Valboa delivered the rather traditional forecast. "If I find you in that man's arms," he screeched, "I'll kill you both!"

God, these amateurs.

Thus when it came time for Consuela to list with the White House secretary the name of the one guest the diva was permitted to invite, why the name Clifford Waxout led all the rest.

Success at the second stage.

As I mentioned at the opening of this journal, there are a considerable number of constraints if one undertakes the assassination of the President of the United States. The record of prior accomplishment in this field indicates that the most successful arrangement is to position oneself within eyeball-to-eyeball contact with the gentleman prior to making him aware of your displeasure. Attendance of the White House recital at which the world's finest soprano had been requested to perform should fulfill the requirement adequately.

Two days to fruition!

The polished parts of the plot intermeshed, spun, hissed in cycles of flawless precision, a thin layer of carefully applied lubricant separating each cog and lever from grinding on its matching component; sweet music to the craftsman. The President, Old '76 himself, returned to Washington from a vacation in Michigan. The concert was officially announced, the guest list published in the Washington Post. They spelled my name correctly. Scott Valboa was not seen or heard from. Sulk on for a few more days, lad. I secured a room for myself in the Prima Donna's hotel. Consuela, Monsieur Brichant, and I dined together on the two evenings prior to the concert. The sly Frenchman excused himself early on both occasions. Consuela appeared grateful to her manager for this gallantry. The good night kisses at the diva's apartment door moved a few inches to the left, from her soft cheek to her softer mouth. I programmed my assault on the dear thing's virtue so as to overrun this tantalizing objective on the day of the recital. The date was to go down in the official history of Mandrell Limited as one of resounding achievement. Go slit your atoms, mein Professors, or harness the oceans, the sun; whatever excites you. For we the laymen, there are happily other specialties available in which we can display stunning accomplishment. Ah, but what of the West Coast? Is all serene there? Quick, Augustus, the telephone.

My barometer of Portland's docility bore the name Fred Hoffman, the man I'd left to oversee the Waxout Empire. A tranquil minute went by in the telephone booth with Fred reporting to me mysterious statistics concerning fan belts and pump packings. Then the poor man broke into a touching tirade regarding the Accounting Department of Waxout Industries. It appears they had refused to honor my verbal agreement (as relayed by Fred) to increase Herr Hoffman's salary.

"Can't you remember where you left the requisition, Mr. Waxout?" he pleaded. "I've searched high and low."

"Oh, yeah, that thing," I said. "This will give you a laugh, Fred. I found the rec. here in my suitcase. Took it with me by mistake. Just as well though, I want to talk to you before I put it through. How bad do you want the $5,000.00, Fred?"

"Well, every man likes to look ahead, Mr. Waxout. I mean, the boy is starting college and—"

"Okay, you'll get the raise. I'll mail the rec. out tonight. But... but, Fred there's a condition. You're going to have to give up your wife. I've had my eye on her for some time now and I want her."

"My *wife!*"

Yes. All 180 pounds of her with her sinus condition and her voice like dry snakeskin. "You'll have to step out of the way, Fred," I advised the thunderstruck gentleman. "And, in return, in addition to the $5,000.00, I'll step out of your way. I know what you and Mrs. Waxout have been up to all these years—all those motel visits."

"Your wife!?" he yelped.

"We'll handle it like civilized men, Fred. When I get back, Friday, I want to find you moved into my place. The house will go to Nell in the divorce anyway. Get over there tonight and talk to her. I imagine sleeping in my bed will be nothing new to you. And for Christ's sake have Wilma (Frau Hoffman) get out and get herself some descent nightgowns. Lots of peek-a-boo stuff. I'll call you tomorrow." Click.

Fred eventually reported to the investigating authorities that I had sounded strange, possibly even "unbalanced" the last time he spoke to me. His address listed in the newspaper accounts at the time was reported as the Portland YMCA."

Fred's conversation, with its self-centered orientation, was comforting. Evidently he still accepted the reality of a hale and hearty, if erratic, employer temporarily on business on the East Coast.

Surely if the Pacific Ocean had prematurely spewed up the cadaver of Clifford Waxout, Fred would have mentioned it; knowing my passion for local gossip.

There appeared no demanding reason to call my portly spouse, Nell. Fred would bring her my salutation. There was cause however to contact Polly Culver. The Secretary of *America's Americans*, Northwest Division would certainly be questioned by the law buffoons. She had to be coached to provide the proper answers. As a matter of fact dear Polly, I suspected, would be subjected to more than mere questioning. There was certain to be some grumbling regarding the issue of "conspiracy" since the American people, despite their impressive history of individual action, appear rather keen on attributing dramatic events, particularly those of an antisocial nature, to shadowy groups. In the flinging out of furious revenge on a national scale one really needs more than a single frail human target. How often can you behead one man? Ah, but I must speak justly here. The human hunger for retribution is hardly an American original. All of us, my children, thirst for a spot of blood now and again.

Thus poor Polly Culver would certainly be dragged into the investigative embryo, probably by the heels. It is hoped that Northwest Division has access to competent legal flim flam. Ten years or so of penal life was certain to impair to some degree Polly's fine appetite for lust. Another national resource depleted. Where will it all end?

"Clifford, I've been waiting for you to call all week," Mrs. Culver squealed. "Just a minute, darling, let me disconnect the recorder plug. I'm sure we don't want our conversation on tape. Oh, Clifford, you naughty boy, I think about you every time I come into the office and see that rug ripped from the floor," she giggled. "But why are you calling from Washington? I thought you were in Baltimore."

"Can't be helped, my dear," I said crisply. "If Operation Fightback is to be initiated Washington is the place to be."

"Operation Fightback? What is it, something to do with your company?"

"No, no, Polly, it has to do with us. With *America's Americans.* Our last ditch weapon you might say. Only a few Directors have been briefed on it so far. I can't tell you any more now except to say that you'll be seeing it in the news."

"You said that the last time you called," she cried. "Clifford, who have you been talking to? Have you seen Crossfox? Clifford, that man is insane. Don't do anything he says!"

"Martin Crossfox," I droned mystically, "Martin J. Crossfox, a patriot and a true friend of the Republic, was parachuted into Russia at 0400 this morning. He is into Operation Fightback up to his dandruff. He carries with him only a telescope-mounted rifle, a simple hand compass, and a pocketful of dried cornmeal. You will be hearing about Martin J. Crossfox too."

"Clifford...my God. Clifford exactly where are you?"

"Sorry, Polly, I've got to hang up. The bastards are surrounding the telephone booth. They're cute, damned cute, dressed up like a pair of nuns. But they forgot one thing. One little slip, but enough for a man with my training. The one nun is carrying a pink poodle. God only knows what's inside that dog."

"Clifford --!"

I hung up. Operation Fightback had no place for hysterical women.

The day of the White House recital was plotted by myself with as much precision as I had devoted to the total commission. With no Scott Valboa about, with his meddling ambitions, and with Monsieur Brichant, and his mania for restricting Madam to her regime, off to New York City, I was successful in persuading Consuela to join me in an early morning drive of the lush Virginia countryside. (Brichant's errand in New York is an issue we will pursue at a later point in this chronicle. For the moment let me mention only that the Frenchman was attempting to schedule a meeting with one Augustus Mandrell of Mandrell Limited. Yes, the same chap; your humble narrator.)

Consuela on this crisp morning was indeed a sight to store in one's memory locket. Seated beside me in the Dodge convertible she was a damned good looking woman. As she responded giddily to the pressure of the wind pressing the fabric of her yellow dress to her body, squeezing the bubbling flow of illicit freedom into her blood. The disciplines of her Prima Donna existence dictated that she spend the morning of so prestigious a performance isolated to her hotel apartment, pinned to a chaise lounge stockpiling her vigor. Her afternoon was to be the property of her masseur; a lady assigned the delightful task of kneading tone into the ligaments that held together the priceless singing machine. There would have been then a light dinner followed by a two-hour nap.

My intention was to decimate at least three quarters of this agenda, all except the period of bed rest. Those two hours I would use well.

The lovely diva had been lured to the Virginia foliage by my description of, "...this ideal bit of a tavern absolutely brimming with Revolutionary War bric-a-brac, sitting almost unnoticed in this short valley, the towering walls of granite at its backyard actually appearing ready to avalanche at any moment." Happily we chanced upon a little log cabin in the Woodbridge area, a cedar roofed bistro with touching delusions of charm that superficially accommodated my description. We sat in the shaded patio and the pulse of our conversation was shaped by the lazy tempo of the hushed woods and the sodden flap of groggy blackbird wings in the trees behind us.

"With the exception of humidity," I said, "this does bring memories of Dr. Salazar's villa just outside Setubal, Portugal. Of course there one must adjust to the enigmatic doctor's habit of permitting his watchdogs—two black leopards—the run of the magnificent grounds. What one must be alert for is some guest that has been too heavily into the amaretto. A reveler will occasionally assume it a bit of a lark to unlock the gates and permit the black beasts access to the house. Quite unsettling to enter your bath and find one of them stretched in your tub."

"I've been meaning to ask you," my luscious companion said, "Pierre was speaking to a friend of his, Ian Ballentine, who is also well known to Picasso. Ian said that he had never heard that Picasso was ever a member of an acrobatic team that swung on a trapeze hanging from an airplane."

I chuckled. "One might wonder how well known Mr. Ballentine is to Picasso. Although in all fairness I will say that Pablo doesn't exactly brag about the period. Painful memories, I suppose. That little actress we dropped over Rouen for instance."

"How dreadful! I suppose she...?"

"No, no, fortunately she fell into this clutch of pigeon coops on the roof of the munitions factory. Well, actually, when we flew down we discovered they were doves. Our concern for the young lady was not only unnecessary—she appeared less absorbed with her injuries than with the advances of some of the more amorous lads in the flock—but also our faith in Benito's skill as a pilot turned out to be ill advised. The Italian managed to somehow swing Pablo and his trapeze smashing into the rubble on the factory rooftop. Then that's rather the lesson learned by all who have put their trust in the hands of Il Duce, eh?"

"Il Duce? You mean Benito Mussolini was your pilot?"

"Rather amusing isn't it, I mean considering our divergent paths since those days? Poor Benito. Pablo gave him such a hard time. He was desperate for Picasso to design him a uniform for this rat pack Benito had collected about himself in the slums of Milan."

"But was Pablo injured when he hit the pigeon coops?"

"No, Pablo retained his grasp on the trapeze cross-bar while Benito brought the aircraft out of the dive. Then, as you may or may not know, Pablo possesses the grip of a gorilla. Anyone who has ever scoured his paintings for any touch of sensitivity or fragility can quickly attest to that. He certainly needed his strength in those moments. The wild doves from the shattered coops were at us with their claws and hungry needle beaks, seeking revenge. Some of the more aggressive pursued us all the way to the landing field."

"And you actually considered a life of aerial acrobatics, Clifford? You and Pablo Picasso?"

"Oh, Consuela, the indiscretions of our youth. No, that was our final performance. Once we landed, there were nearly fisticuffs between Pablo and our Neapolitan pilot. Benito was absolutely distraught. On a man-to-man comparison, you know, physical combat, I suspect the pugnacious Italian might have prevailed. But he desperately wanted the prestige of a Picasso design for his army of malcontents. There I was attempting to keep them separated; Picasso full of Spanish outrage, Benito sobbing that Pablo had promised the design. As Pablo turned away to the automobile parking lot he tore off his shirt and threw it in Benito's face. 'There,' he cried, 'there is your uniform. It is appropriate.' Benito stared at the brown shirt and muttered, 'At least it will match their eyes.' Actually I'm certain Pablo was referring to the blood stains on the garment."

"There were blood stains?"

"Pablo's blood," I said. "Where one of the doves had dived beak first into the back of Pablo's head. I'm afraid our noble Spaniard brooded over his wounds at the villa all evening. Next morning Pablo and his friend Mahatma returned to the coops with shotguns and slaughtered the entire flock. A man with an instinct for vengeance to be sure."

"Pablo and his friend, who...?"

And thus did our delightful lunch wend its way into the soft afternoon. Eventually the time arrived for forward progress in my intentions. "I must be getting you back to Washington, my sweet," I said at about one o'clock.

"Oh, Clifford, how I wish there were no concert tonight. What a lovely, happy day. Must it end?" This blasphemy Consuela spoke as we rolled among the scented hills, inhaling on the crest of the Schmidt Divide not the residual exhaust gases from our fellow motorists but rather, and I know not why, the insane odor from the leafy compost in the Virginia fields.

I swung the Dodge onto a horse-trailer path outside Leesburg, and along the white-fenced meadows of the Austin Ranch until we emerged on a bluff overlooking the mist-shrouded Potomac River Valley. Easing from the car I took Consuela's hand and said, "Yes, my sweet, the day must end. But there is much of it left yet. Come, let us smother our senses in this earthy wine."

Was it the design built into the vehicle by the Chrysler engineers or was it the guile of the female? As Consuela slid toward me across the front seat the skirt of her light dress pulled tight about her splendid thighs. Ah, does it matter how or who? The man was smitten. Instead of permitting her to complete her exit I held her to the edge of the front seat with pressure from my hand holding hers. I let the diva see my eyes flail over her full legs, encircling and compressing them with the leverage of a hay rake. I swayed in the heat of the sun. I very nearly fell toward the DiMartino, on top of her. I regained control over my stunned limbs an instant before Consuela's white lips released my frightened name.

We strolled in skittish silence from the car to a long arch formed by leafy birches. The hand in mine trembled. We looked silently into the Potomac River Valley. When I raised Consuela's face to mine with my fingers under her chin her lips had regained their color and ripe inflation. And there was minimal rigidity in her thighs when I pressed them against a smooth silver birch with my own thighs. Our long kiss was stoked by our intermeshing tongues and the exotic flavor of her lipstick.

Ah, but there are moments the Gods deliver to us and we frequently have not the wit to recognize their precious, fleeting structure. How many times over the years have I regretted the decision made that afternoon by the fastidious Mr. Mandrell, the decision to forgo the perfectly adequate confines of the back seat of the Dodge convertible. He was confidently aiming for the plush cloister of the lady's hotel apartment. Has the archer's eye ever been so sadly erratic?

The magic flush of Consuela's near encounter with the long-awaited deflowering was still running loose in my dame when we reached the hotel. As we approached her door, there was some foolishly poignant sense in the clasped hands and the quick glances of, 'this has never happened to anybody else before.'

"I suppose..." I stammered, "I suppose I will not see you again until we are ready to leave for the concert?" There was need to test the woof of her passion.

"Couldn't we dine together, Clifford? It will be a bit early but..."

"Ah, let me think....What is your schedule like after you eat?"

"Oh an hour or so of rest, after my bath. Why?"

"And your maid will be in attendance of course?"

There was a pause, as well there should be. A pause during which the restraint of a lifetime had to be assessed. Should or should not this over-nourished restraint be toppled? Had the undermining of the staid foundation by the nervous digger been sufficiently deep? Or would it be necessary to bring in the sappers?

"I...I could send Maria someplace, Clifford."

"I'll be here at 5:30," I breathed. "Just after your bath," Another kiss in the foyer of the apartment. The hot wax seal on our decision.

I fled to my own room six floors above. One hour was available to me. One hour in which to polish the final pieces of the ritual. It would then be 5:30, the hour in which I would collect my charming bonus. At 7:00 Consuela and I would depart for the White House. At 8:00 the Prima Donna would be presented to the President and his guests. Her accompanist would strike the opening piano chords. The diva would sing. At 8:15....

As I bathed and dressed in my room did I actually detect some essence of the beautiful woman preparing herself in the apartment several floors below? I have discovered during my savory career that as the moment of culmination draws close my senses strip themselves to a response time of hypercritical intensity. There is a limit of course. I cannot, as some of my more hysterical critics insist, peer through stonewalls.

The available hour passed swiftly. There was the gun to clean. You'll recall Clifford Waxout purchased the weapon just prior to departing Portland, Oregon. There was the literature from the printing presses of *America's Americans* to scatter about the room. Most of these leaflets were from the latest run issued by Northwest Division Titled, *Communism Is Okay –If You Are A Communist Slave And Have Forgotten How To Fight For Liberty.* On the borders of several of these sheets I had appended some provocative notes, thoughts that had overcome me during my stay in Washington, D.C.

There was: TO WEED OUT THE EVIL OF COMMUNISM WE MUST START AT THE TOP. Somewhat irrefutable, I'd say. One of my favorites was: OUR LEADERS ARE LYING TO US TO PROTECT THEIR OWN SECRETS. NOBODY CAN TELL ME 800 MILLION CHINESE BECAME COMMUNISTS OVER NIGHT. THERE HAD TO BE MONEY, TOP NOTCH MANAGEMENT, AND AMERICAN KNOW-HOW. OUR LEADERS HAVE SOLD US DOWN THE YANGZEE RIVER.

And then the crux of the thing: THE PRESIDENT IS THE CAPTAIN OF THE SHIP OF STATE. WHEN THE SHIP IS HEADED INTO THE WRONG PORT—A GODLESS PORT WHERE WHITE AMERICAN MOTHERS WILL BECOME THE PLAYTHINGS OF BEARDED ASIANS WITH BODY ODOR—THEN EVERY LOYAL AMERICAN MUST FIGHT TO TURN THE SHIP AROUND. IF THIS BE MUTINY? THEN GIVE ME MUTINY OR GIVE ME DEATH.

Here and there on the leaflets, I scattered some illustrations for those who did not have time to read the complete text; severally crudely drawn skull-and-crossbones logos.

All in all rather maximum grist for the prosecuting attorney and the testimony by his "expert psychologist."

5:30!

I will admit my rush to my door was rather headlong. Perhaps that is why I had the portal full open before I realized that my passage was blocked by a tall grinning idiot. Scott Valboa was standing in the corridor just outside the door. It required more than an instant for me to recognize the ass. He wore a soiled dark trench coat belted about the middle, a black beret, a black turtleneck sweater, and black tennis shoes. Where the hell was he going?

With a flourish that testified to his years of exposure to opera's blatant on-stage posturing, the young man drew a frightful looking revolver from inside the trench coat. He moved toward me, his grin not losing on ounce of its asinine intensity. Needless to say I did not dispute the lad's passage.

"Thought you'd sneak down to her apartment and have yourself a time, didn't you?" He leered, forcing me back with the cavernous nose of the gun. "I saw her maid, Maria, leave just now," he hissed. "I know what you're after. Well here's what you're going to get."

The idiot! The galloping nincompoop! He gave every appearance of being about to actually discharge the firearm!

"Who...?" I stuttered. "Why, it's you Scott! Scott, thank God you're here!" I collapsed back upon a chair, my every ligament expressing my relief that he, Scott, was finally here, thank God.

My greater histrionics were directed, however, toward pretending to ignore the revolver. I said, "We've had the police, the FBI, the Coast Guard, everybody looking for you Scott. Consuela... she keeps calling your name..." The incautious alignment of the gun's snout with my breast slackened slightly. "—How she has lasted this long, nobody knows. The knife blade is actually into her heart but we're afraid to remove it—" He paled. "—She still clings to that last thread of life and repeats over and over, Scott, Scott, Scott..." My hands covered my face and grotesque sobs shook my complete carcass.

"Where is she?" He screamed. "Where is she?"

I pointed limply at the locked door to the adjacent room.

"Consuela..." he cried and ran toward the door.

I catapulted from my chair, used the bed in front of me as a trampoline, and landed knees first, into the center of his back. He was driven head first into the door he sought. I knifed two fingers into his neck pinching, at the pedicle, just the correct vertebrae nerves. He was unconscious. For an instant I considered the advantages of killing him.

No Mr. Valboa, you shall live. You will be another of those bizarre ingredients in the background of Clifford Waxout. There will be a two-fold need for your testimony. You will add credibility to Monsieur Brichant's testimony and the Diva's that they had no knowledge of this scoundrel, Clifford Waxout, prior to his appearance in your lives at Whitman's Restaurant. But more important, my lad, you are essential to establishing Consuela's culpability. The Diva's defense attorney, surely a man knowledgeable in human frailty will be retained, must keep you on the stand for the necessary hours to draw out your capacity for dullness, pettiness, and boredom. The jurors, in particular the lady jurors, must have sufficient exposure to your charm, lad, to conclude: God yes, I'd take a chimpanzee to the recital before I'd take this dummy."

Only you, Scott, can convince the jury of Consuela's total innocence. I can hear you now, lad, on the stand, righteousness in every syllable: "I told Miss DiMartino time and time again this fellow Waxout was up to no good. But, do you think Miss DiMartino listened? No, she thought I was jealous. Jealous of that bald-headed smarty pants, can you imagine that?" Excellent, Scott.

So Scott Valboa was to be forgiven his minor intrusion into my master plan. He would live. The stab in the neck would keep him unconscious for two to three hours, unless someone administered him a stimulant. Were any of the hotel lackeys due to visit my room? The hostelry was one of those stately old Washington institutions that believed in pampering the guests; plugging in the false fireplace and turning down the bed in the evening once they caught your back turned. Then, too, had Valboa told any friends of his impetuous agenda? Would they follow the lad to measure his success?

Gadfrey, the buffoon had to be made unavailable.

Since he had appeared so intent on the room next door, why not provide him access? I am not above a charitable act now and again.

During my residence in the hotel I had noted no indication that the adjacent room was occupied. An ideal storage bin for the brash Mr.Valboa. I manipulated the door's latching device with a bit of steel from my notecase until the portal swung open, revealing of course another door back-to-back with the door I'd just opened. For what is a descent hotel if not a labyrinth of impacted isolation?

The second door fell before my pick and I ushered the limp form within. My assumption regarding the absence of a neighbor was incorrect. Scattered about the room were several items of dress indicating residence by a male lodger. The untidy gentleman, however, was not receiving. To forestall any blunt encounter between the guest and Mr. Valboa (you'll recall they had not been introduced) I induced Scott to seek the shelter of the rug beneath the bed.

Late, late!

I returned to my room, kicked Scott's wretched gun under the sofa, and ran for the corridor. Ah, my patient prize, I am on my way.

The elevator was just coming to a halt at my floor. A minor shift in the winds of the luck of Augustus Mandrell? Yes, a shift indeed. But in which insidious direction?

Out of the elevator stepped a harried matron in search of base adventure. Her passions had whipped across 3,000 miles of the United States and she came tumbling from the elevator in a froth.

"Clifford!" she cried as her eye nailed mine. "Clifford, what a terrible time I've had finding you."

Great horned toads of despair—Polly Culver!

"You have the advantage of me, dear lady," I said stiffly, as I slipped an arm into the elevator and pressed the desired button.

Inside the car was another passenger, a small man of fifty odd years squeezed in a corner taking embarrassed refuge behind a gray homburg.

"Clifford..." Polly's unbelieving voice cried.

"I warn you," I continued sternly to Polly (when would the damn door close?) "I am not your average unwary traveler. I have rejected overtures similar to yours in many a world port. Hong Kong, Singapore, Bombay—"

The door finally started to close. Waiting until the last second, I leapt nimbly aboard the car. Ha, but Polly proved equal to the game. She rammed her arm between the door and its jam. The door, dumb, docile lowsuit-oriented slug that it was, halted, hissed in shocked alarm and then backed up.

Polly came aboard like a buccaneer on to a captured galleon, "Clifford, Clifford, what's the matter? It's me." She had my arm gripped into her soft solar plexus.

Now the fool door closed fully and the elevator started upward. Perhaps at the next stop I could toss her out into the corridor. "My good woman," I said patiently, "must you persist in this obvious commercial venture? I am much too otherwise occupied this evening. Perhaps this other gentleman has ten minutes or so he can devote to your...?"

It was no use. The damned vehicle proceeded upward. Polly's grip on my arm became more feral. Bone-ribbed determination broiled in her eye. Retreat, Augustus, retreat.

"Good Lord," I exclaimed and put my fingers to my eyes to clear them, "Polly Culver! My dear, what brings you to the nation's capital this time of year?"

"I've been looking for you all day," Polly fairly screeched. "All over the city. Her grip on her composure was not near as firm as the talon clutch at my arm.

The car came to a halt at the 18th floor. The little man attempted to scuttle past us. No, no, my dear sir, you are not leaving me trapped in an elevator with a hysterical woman. We shall exit here and we are certainly not in need of an escort of your obvious gossipy mien.

"Back, back, you cur," I cried, leveling a rigid finger at the gentleman. He lurched back into his corner. "It did not escape my attention, sir," I accused holding the door open with one hand and urging Polly out with the pressure of my trapped arm, "that a moment ago you outraged this lady. When I inquired about the availability of your private organs for the lady's pleasure, you were about to deny her access to same." Polly and I were in the corridor.

I released the elevator door. As it closed I flung my final gauntlet at the cowering brute. "I can only regret that you are not half my size, sir. Were you I would certainly have smitten you."

The elevator took the coward away, downward. Downward toward the floor of my dreadfully elusive Nirvana. Consuela, Consuela...

Ignoring Polly's joyless blabber I led the way to the fire stairs on the 18th floor. When my companion saw the dingy, naked-cement stairway, she cried, "Stop, stop. Where in heaven's name are we going?"

"I presumed you would want to visit my room," I leered. With its closet and bathroom, each with a door, either an acceptable repository for about 125 pounds of superfluous flesh.

"Ohhh, what a naughty suggestion, Clifford, what kind of a girl do you think I am? And those awful things you said in the elevator. I'm not sure a girl is safe with you. You have a roguish eye, Clifford..." And on and on, this drivel, while we made our way down the fire stairs and achieved my room on the 16th floor.

As I unlocked the door, Polly said, "What did you mean on the telephone, Clifford? What was that talk about Operation Fightback?"

I inspected her eye. My, how quickly the immoral ingénue had been elbowed aside by the cold-blooded Secretary of *America's*

Americans, Northwest Division, this hotel room tumbling will be fine and dandy, Mr. Director, but first let's find out how much of a bloody fool you've been. Ah, you ladies, you are indeed indomitable.

"My dear," I said, as I fiddled with latching the door on the inside, "is that the water in the bath I hear? Would you be good enough to see if I left it running?"

I had turned away from her, presenting my back in the event she were inclined to balk at the mission I had assigned. Therefore, her scream, a grotesque spear of sound, struck the back of my head with shocking impact.

I spun to her and found she was rooted to the floor just past the bed. Her eyes were popped staring at the portion of the rug that was blocked from my view by the bed. She staggered back toward the wall, gulping for breath, her pointed finger leaving a promised trail of horror on the rug.

I eased to her side of the room, my hand under my dinner jacket curled about warm steel. Would this infamous day never end?

Scott Valboa lay on the rug next to the bed. What demonic mind had designed the young man's cast iron nervous system? How dare this soft-brained lout continue to plague me?

The lad appeared to be senseless. But how then had he escaped the neighboring room? Scuttling about with appropriate craven caution I managed to test the boy's heart and pulse. Each of these plumbing complex gauges indicated the sluggish tom-tom of a near mummified state. Was he feigning? Had he somehow roused himself from the wicked slumber I had induced, crawling from the adjoining room to this location, then swooned again? There was one dependable test remaining.

Grasping him in a frantic grip I tossed his unwelcome body upon the bed and directed the light into his eyes. The orbs reflected back the unchanging dilation of temporary relief of all the burdens of consciousness. The lad was not faking. He was as bereft of his faculties as he had been when I left him. How then had he...?

"Clifford, who is he?" Polly croaked. "Is he...is he...er...injured?"

"Let us hope so, my dear. Take a good look at that face and pray that you never see it again as long as you live." The enormity of my disclosure so staggered me that I moved backwards away from the evil thing on the bed. My travel took me up against the door to the room next door. My hand behind my back found the knob. The door was locked.

"But, who is he?"

"He's the man they call Mr. Potomac Poleax. A very special FBI agent. Assigned to the very secret group called the Ultimate Weapon Squad. Assassins all. Note the double cleft in his chin? Congressional sanction authorizing him to kill at the drop of a hat."

"Our FBI has such people? The American FBI?"

"This means they've found us," I said a bit frantic. "The battle has been enjoined."

"All right, Clifford, I want some answers," Polly said, her backbone snapping to a rigid, inflexible line of efficiency. The line extended to her jaw. "You've evaded me long enough. You avoid every question I ask about your activities here in Washington. You will please explain yourself right now!" By God, but she was made of well-tempered alloys.

"Certainly, my dear, certainly. But I must contact Colonel Subrosa, first, find out how close they are." I snatched up the phone and spouted the number of a room on the third floor; any number. While the switchboard operator was ringing the room, I said to Polly, "Colonel Subrosa is here in the hotel. He has people watching the lobby. Don't worry we're prepared."

"Who the hell is Colonel Subrosa?" The steel-trap secretary demanded. "Somebody from the Middle-Atlantic Division. One of those idiots. Clifford I—"

A timid female voice had answered in my ear from the third floor with a leery, "Hello."

"Hello Colonel," I snapped, interrupting Polly, "This is Blacksheep-One. How goes it with Operation Fightback?"

"This is Eunice," the timid voice said, "is this the fella Polly told me about?"

I stammered, "They're in the hotel? Surrounded...!?" I dropped the telephone, my fingers overtaken by an icy spasm. I removed a portion of blood from my head. My face took on the proper whitish cast to support my concern.

"They're on the way up!" I cried to Polly. "They caught Colonel Subrosa's mother in the lobby and beat her with truncheons until she confessed the room numbers. Colonel Subrosa could hardly speak. He's taken his suicide pill. C'mon, there isn't a moment to lose. We'll head for the roof."

I flung open the door to the corridor determined to haul my shapely but embarrassing burden to the roof or basement, anyplace, and lose her. To think, to think! of the embrace awaiting me on the tenth floor, the embrace of a princess, and here I wander, I with this single-minded peasant. By God, into the elevator she goes whether the car is there or not!

I paused in the corridor to lock the door to my room, seal off Scott Valboa. As I gave the knob a last test to ensure poor Scott would not be disturbed, a male voice from behind me said, "Never mind locking it, buddy." There was a dreadful poundage of authority in the voice, as though...as though my glib fantasy concerning the FBI agents from the lobby...

I turned carefully and faced two men. One, the speaker, I did not know. The other was the slight, homburged idiot who had ridden in the elevator with Polly and me.

The hefty stranger spoke again. "Dr. Glover here tells me you folks spoke to him in the elevator. Made him what might be called an interesting proposition." Ah, what is a home without a built-in detective?

"Dr. Glover," the flatfoot continued, "he says you, mister, offered this lady's services to him and when he turned them down you threatened him with bodily harm. Now, this hotel don't cotton too much to our permanent guests being threatened in the elevators." (Where then, pray tell?)

He was a wide, deep-chested man, this detective, with eyes that bespoke craft and competence.

"Also," Mr. Detective continued spilling his cornucopia of ill tidings, "a sorta wild looking guy in a trench coat and beret was hanging around the lobby earlier. He snuck upstairs about a half hour ago and got off at this floor. So, like I said, Mr. Waxout—if you are Mr. Waxout—don't bother locking your door. I want a little look around."

My eye ran over this custodian of transient tranquility, gauging his possible resilience to physical assault. He scaled out at about 2 ¼ pounds heavier than the minimal prudent requirement for such action; the critical poundage in residence in a leather pouch strapped under his arm. Ah well, back to the weapons of civilized Man, guile and deceit.

"Are you a medical doctor?" I said breathlessly to Dr. Glover, the pipsqueak tattletale. "I mean, not horses and orangutan and the like?"

"Certainly I am a medical doctor," he asserted, drawing his chin up with rather a fetching dignity. "But just because I am very familiar with the human body—I mean, I do treat female patients and do recognize what those various openings are for..." He glanced frightened at Polly for a second, and then stammered on. "I am not and never have been open to immoral propos...er, suggestions, I assure you. I am a healer of the flesh not a ...er..."

"Good, good," I said eagerly and grasped his hand to shake it. "There will be need of your skills momentarily, sir. But first—" I took the detective's arm and urged him toward the other side of the corridor. "The hotel is in desperate trouble," I whispered, the lever to nudge him along with me.

"Waddya mean?" he whispered back.

"I don't know what to do with her," I lamented (painful truth.)

"She's insatiable. Forever making these lewd proposals to any man she meets."

"You mean the lady?" the flatfoot whispered.

I nodded. "Don't stare at her. Please! She'll start undressing right here. That other man you mentioned—with the beret? She must have found the poor guy here in the corridor. Or maybe she encouraged him to meet her here, I don't know. That's how she usually operates. Anybody. Truck drivers, delivery boys, garbage men, bartenders..."

"But who is she? Your...your wife?"

"No, no. The wife of a good friend. He's at the Pentagon, an Admiral with a career to protect. I...I try to help out. Drain some of the excess energy. But she needs a regiment, a cellblock! You should see what she did to that guy in the beret. Drained like a toothpaste tube..."

"Well, you know, guys that wear berets...?" the trained psychologist offered.

"Evidently," I concurred. "Anyway, he's in there now, out cold on my bed. I came back from dinner and found them. Isn't there anything we can do? Would it be possible...? I hate to ask, but could you possibly escort her off someplace and reason with her? Someplace quiet?"

It is not often that a man is treated to the sight of unbridled lust bursting from another man's eye. The display is normally reserved for dark rooms. My house dick measured Polly Culver's ripe body from the corner of his eye. He blinked several times, possibly to dam the draining passion. Perhaps he knew he'd best stockpile for the upcoming onslaught on his vital juices.

"I...I guess I could talk to her down in my office," he said thickly.

"I wish you would," I said. "Perhaps the doctor can help."

"Naw," he said shaking his head, his eyes now full on Polly's trim bosom. "I can handle her alone, Mr. Waxout. Never met a dame, er, lady, I couldn't..."

"I meant the doctor might administer her a sedative. She's not due home until morning. God knows how much mischief she'll get into if...if..." My voice broke.

"That's all right sir, take it easy now. Yeah, I'll get the doctor's help if I need it."

I grasped his hand and nodded my humble thanks to this reservoir of strength. To Polly I sent a reassuring, conspiratorial wink. If you will keep that pretty mouth shut for but a few seconds more, my dear.

"I am desperately late," I said to the cop with the proper tone of urgency. "Good luck with her."

I turned my back on them, on their mixed bag of ambitions, and walked quickly toward the elevator bank. Consuela...

"Hey, wait a minute, Mr. Waxout," the detective called. "You'd better unlock your door first. I've got to get the guy in the beret outta there. He ain't a registered guest."

You slope-headed robot idiot! Oh, is it any wonder that the Gods do despair of Man? They lash out at him not in anger but in disappointment.

To hesitate at this moment would be to distract, a balk in the twirling cape work. "Oh, of course," I said and hurried back to them. "Don't worry, my dear," I said to Polly, pressing on her a secret, burlesqued wink. "These men are friends. They are going to help us."

Dr. Glover, honed to impatience by the evident rapport between myself and the law, started to sputter. "Help you with what, sir? I am not—"

The nice detective dropped a hand on the doctor's shoulder and squeezed in some assurance regarding justice and retribution.

I unlocked the door. While I was having that bit of trouble extracting my key I opened the door wide to the sheep. Their leader said, "All right, folks, let's all go on in. Don't want anybody wandering off by herself." He had his hand pressing lightly on the center of Polly's shoulders, the hand of ownership, the breeder pawing the stock. They filed into the room past me.

At the sight of Scott Valboa on the bed the lawman and the doctor were both professionally actuated. They moved in on the unconscious lad to assess the level of mayhem/disease contained in the carcass. It is possible that in their dedication to their crafts they did not note for several seconds that the distinguished Mr. Waxout was not in residence, had remained in the corridor after closing the door. How long it took them to discover the slender strip of plastic jammed in the door's locking mechanism I have no idea. It is certain only that they did not immediately find the plastic, for while it remained in the lock the door could not be opened, not by any normal exertion. One hopes that the three gentlemen and the tense lady from Portland, Oregon found some sweet reverie to occupy them during my absence. Perhaps Polly is well overdue for an annual physical. Has that occurred to you, Dr. Glover? You paranoid ass.

I rushed to Consuela, late. Dreadfully late.

Consuela, dressed in a fur-trimmed lounging robe, opened her door to me. "Clifford, what happened? You said 5:30. It's nearly seven. I couldn't imagine...I'm afraid I even tried to call your room. The line was busy." Ah, my call to Colonel Subrosa.

"My poor darling," I said, steering her delightful body toward the large chaise lounge. "Some fantastic call from Oregon, from my factory. An explosion. Twenty men blown to bits. I had to talk to the wives and mothers, of course. Terrible, terrible mess." I shook my head to clear the searing picture of stark tragedy from my brain.

"Darling, how awful. Is there anything I can do?"

"Yes, my sweet," I murmured, smiling with effort. "Help an old man forget for the few minutes we have."

"Ahh, my poor Clifford. Will this help you forget?" She opened her robe slowly. Underneath she wore a transparent peignoir. White of course. Beneath this lovely curtain she wore only a birthmark or two.

Advance, Augustus, and serve thyself.

I slid my arms around her and gently pressed the absolutely desirable Consuela to me. We fell, as naturally as two innocent animals, to the chaise lounge. The woman, this woman that was now mine, shuddered and trembled beneath my hand.

"Clifford," her whisper licked my ear like a flame. "Clifford, don't you want to go to my bedroom? It is ready. I am..."

Oh those swine! Those blundering swine upstairs in my room! What have they done to me? Was ever a mortal so cheated?

"I want nothing less, my darling," I whispered. Consuela stirred on the lounge preparing to rise. I held her back. "My sweet," I said, "we cannot. There isn't time. Those damned phone calls have spoiled it. The car from the White House will be here in thirty minutes. I want hours and hours with you."

"Oh darling, no," she wailed and gripped at me with every fiber that could be brought to bear. God, Consuela...

I released my caution, had it torn from me by the flood of soft flesh. For a few minutes I allowed Consuela to swamp my senses in a warm lagoon of roiling musk.

Bit by bit, slender unbreakable thread by undeniable thread, my implacable, insensitive brain reeled me in, back to insufferable duty. A house detective was prowling my room six floors above my head. He and the wretched doctor must have discovered by now that Scott Valboa could not be roused. The quack had had some training one presumes. Some alarmed inquiry was surely in progress.

The discovery of Valboa's revolver under the bed, full of bullets I imagine, would remove the incident from Mr. Detective's specialized arena. A gun and an unconscious body equated: get the police. One speculated on what conclusions the Washington Police Department might draw when confronted with the *America's Americans'* pamphlets found scattered about the room. Dear Polly could explain the basic text of the documents, but these exuberant notes appended in the margins, what would the flatfeet think of those?

One had damn well find out what the law chaps thought of them.

But at what an incredible price!

I pulled the passion-stoked body from me. We came unstuck with dreadful effort. I drew a smile from God knows where. "My Consuela, get dressed now, my darling. I'll meet you at the limousine stop. Hold the White House car there for a few minutes if I'm late."

There was resistance in my lovely Diva, a female unwillingness to stop. Her wet, half opened mouth came after mine. I did not believe I could survive if ever she dragged me down again into her terrible lair. I swiftly uncoiled from the lounge, away from the tigress.

"Oh, darling," she moaned. "Yes, yes you are right of course. We'll have so much time together later. Hours. Days. Bring me home immediately after the recital, Clifford, I'll accept only two bows. Absolutely only two."

Oh, you witch, do not twist the dagger!

One last look at her, at the shocking loss. She saw my eye and bestirred herself on the lounge with wicked effect. "Help dress me, Clifford," she breathed. She may have been untried and brimming with fear, but by Caesar she was game!

Ah, my darling, if only this night's toil were not so committed to a precise schedule. If only the fee for same were not so equitable with the artist's skill, with Augustus Mandrell's finest effort, with any sacrifice...

In that moment, staring down at her displayed in a billow of cloth, I knew why I had earlier spared Scott Valboa a second jab in the neck. This young, untouched animal before me was to spend the greater portion of the night ahead crouched under the foul interrogation of howling, frightened men. These were fools who did not know a Prima Donna from the proprietress of a bordello. And once the notice of my deed of the evening had been released, the official lust for vengeful carnage in public-oriented Washington, D.C. would sway more sanity then the name DiMartino could hope to rally.

Who then would preserve this priceless animal? Was it Machiavelli who said: "Gents, find me a scapegoat and we'll all be off the hook?" As the person who brought the assassin to the White House, escorted him into that very private house under her wing, as such Consuela would be the interim scapegoat. Who would speak for her?

Pierre Brichant, of course, would describe how the diva had been deceived and betrayed by the scoundrel, Clifford Waxout. Witness for the defense Brichant's testimony would be noted but his position as Consuela's manager carried with it built-in, commercially oriented cancellation.

What was needed was a defense a jury could sink its emotional teeth into. Thus, the testimony of the anguished innocent, the broken-hearted suitor was required to sprinkle the defense with maudlin, succulent, credulity. The vengeful sewer stuffing would trample anything less and my Consuela would be under.

I leave you this then, my sweet Consuela; the bumbling, but as the god's would have it, loquacious Mr. Scott Valboa.

Ah, Augustus, you old softie.

I grabbed Consuela's wrist and pulled her gently to her feet. "I cannot trust myself to help you dress, my sweet," I said. "We would never reach the White House."

I pushed her toward her bedroom, dispatching her with a quiet slap on what one music critic, another observant chap, has described as, "The most dramatic derriere in all of opera."

"Go, go now and cover some of that awesome beauty," I said, "lest you ignite our President to lechery." She went wistfully to her bedroom and closed the door slowly.

Let us be off, Augustus, there is madness loose in this hotel tonight.

Certainly Scott Valboa would be indispensable on the morrow in the role of Consuela's one believable witness but on this evening he was a loose, high-voltage cable flailing in the dark, crackling and arcing, in search of a warm body through which to ground his electrical charge. (Or do I sell you short, my son?)

Mr. Valboa was privy to one devastating fact not available to any of the other trespassers roaming my room on the 16th floor. Scott knew that Clifford Waxout was scheduled to be at the White House this evening. I have never been overly impressed by the young man's grip on reticence. Should the police succeed in rousing Scott the dazed lad would undoubtedly spout some churlish index of invective against Clifford Waxout, including the childish accusation that I had usurped his rightful place at the President's concert.

There was just the possibility that the tired fuzz would fall from some dormant police brain just long enough for the idiot to join the two pieces; my visit to the White House and the blasphemous pamphlets scattered in the room. Mr. Valboa's testimony had to be discredited.

Before leaving Consuela's room, that empty nest, I called the hotel operator and requested Dr. Glover's room. "I can't remember the number," I said anxiously. "1824 or 1828, something like that."

"1802," the dear thing said helpfully. "I'll ring it for you, sir." A woman answered the doctor's telephone. "Mrs. Glover?" I asked. "Yes, this is Mrs. Glover. Can I help you?" The humanitarian question, with a highly polished surface.

"This is Lieutenant O'Keefe of the police department," I said. "Has the Doc been in touch with you about this case yet?"

"You mean the man here in the hotel? Yes, Doctor returned a moment ago for his bag. He has gone back to his patient though."

His patient? You meddling quack, that unfortunate lad in room 1616 is under the care of none other than Dr. Augustus Mandrell. How dare you tamper with the practice of this internationally known physician.

"Good, good," I said to the doctor's wife. "The Doc told me he was going to get his bag but I didn't know if he had gotten it yet. Do you know if he picked up the extra supply of Nembutal?"

"I don't know. Doctor just ran in and grabbed his case. There should be some vials in the case."

"Hell no...sorry M'am...but that ain't enough. I've got me two of my policemen shot up here in the basement and the leg amputation up in the lobby. We gotta have more Nembutal. Does the Doc keep any more up there in your apartment?'

"Why, yes. But for an amputation you need—"

"I'll be right up," I snapped. "I can't stand to see my boys in pain." Don't worry, lads, your lieutenant hasn't forgotten your loyal service to the Crown...or whatever cloak it is you use to cover your rifling of the taxpayers' note case.

The elevator whisked me to the high altitude pharmacy on the 18th floor. Mrs. Glover, a corseted woman with blue hair dyed to match the frames of her eyeglasses, showed me the doctor's cache of medicines with some reluctance. She was not unaware of the taut relationship between drugs and policemen that has emerged since the advent of hypodermic relief from civic responsibility.

My formal costume too was an added distraction for Frau Glover; a police lieutenant on duty in tails? "I'll bet I miss half the corrida at the Mall tonight because of this mess," I muttered as I pawed the drawer of boxed medications.

I grabbed up two 20cc vials of Nembutal. From a hook by the door I grabbed also a white smock and a surgical mask. "Shouldn't there be some sort of a receipt for this, Lieutenant?" Mrs. Glover asked wisely as I led the way toward the corridor door.

"Good God, lady, my men are bleeding to death!" I dashed from the apartment.

On the way down the fire stairs to my room on the 16th floor I squeezed into the under-sized smock and dropped the gauze mask over the adventurous features of Clifford Waxout.

The door to my lodgings, room 1616, had been removed from its hinges. It is hoped, gentlemen, that you launched the unsealing of my castle in accordance with the proper judicial processes. I'm not certain that the garbled entreaties from the four souls locked therein can be regarded as sufficient justification for this highhanded approach to my property rights. Were there more time at our disposal a courtroom embroilio, complete with robed ignorance, would surely be in order. Ah well...

A gaggle of hotel lackeys stood near the uncovered opening, passively ignoring the tepid entreaties of the two uniformed policemen stationed at the portal to disperse.

"Is this where he is?" I asked the coppers through my gauze mask as I shouldered my way roughly past the rabble. "Is this 1616? Where the hell is the door with the room number?" I did not wait for answers. One doesn't.

The policemen parted before me, before the authority of the surgical mask and the immaculate, blood-free gown.

(Note: The operating room costume is one of the better disguises available in the art of flim flam. With its queasy aura of last-hope, final judgment, it vibrates an uneasy reminder in the belfry of one's life clock, if you will. Are you taking notes?)

There were two old acquaintances in my hotel room and four strangers. Dr. Glover was by the bed holding one of Scott Valboa's eyeballs uncovered with his thumb and peering at the lad's innermost secrets with a pinpoint light. Inquisitive vulture. Two of the strangers were uniformed officer-level members of the D.C. police department. The other two strangers, to judge by their harassed impotence, were management-level coolies from the hotel staff.

Only Dr. Glover was immune to the authority of my costume. Do greasy coveralls awe the blacksmith?

"Your ambulance is downstairs, Doctor," I said somewhat breathlessly and with slight emphasis on the word "your." And if you want a complete hospital emergency room set up at your elbow, good doctor, why a snap of the fingers will engage the required machinery.

When Glover glanced at me his eyes hung on my mask. I tugged the side of the gauze and said, "I've got an 833 count of strep running. Should be in bed but what the hell when you're understaffed..."

He nodded with that genuine sympathy that doctors reserve for each other's illnesses. But, there was too, that slightly embarrassed duck of the head, as though we had somehow failed each other. He returned to lavishing his, presumed, healing powers upon Scott Valboa. The crackpot may have actually remained awake during the University lectures. The lad on the bed was already mumbling and groaning. Ah, Dr. Glover, it is obviously time to fix your meat wagon.

Behind me a comforting medicine was applied to my real affliction: the coppers and the hotel managers had resumed their conversation.

"Where's the woman?" The D.C. police lieutenant asked. "Didn't Peters tell me there was a dame in the room when they found this jerk in the trench coat?"

"Yes, sir," the sergeant answered. "Marv Simon, that's the hotel dick, he took her down to his office. Her name's Polly Culver, just into D.C. today from Portland, Oregon. She got mean when my men broke in here. Said she wasn't going to be tortured by any FBI Goon Squad. She wasn't going to eat any suicide pill. We don't know what she's talking about."

"I don't understand why the hotel's security officer has to be responsible for this Mrs. Culver," one of the managers squeaked. "She isn't even registered."

"Maybe you ought to take that up with your security officer," the sergeant said nasty. "He wouldn't let nobody near the dame. Said he could get something out of her if he has her alone for a while. How's his sex life going lately?"

The complaining manager looked away from the uncouth sergeant.

"Just where the hell does that leave us?" the lieutenant asked his sergeant. "Do you know this house dick?"

"I've got Patrolman Peters with him," the sergeant answered respectfully. "Standing right outside his office."

"Is it really necessary to have so many uniformed police in the lobby?" the other manager, the one with the crew-cut hair, asked. "Couldn't we have plainclothesmen?"

"You can have a brass band and three singing baboons if you want," the Lieutenant said. "If old Uncle Joe Mulrooney didn't own this hotel you'd have to look hard to find a couple of rookies in your lobby. Influence comes in funny packages. Okay, what about this guy, Clifford Waxout? How sure are we that he's still in the hotel?"

"Looks like a good bet," the Sergeant said. "The hotel dick, Marv Simon, called the desk as soon as he found out Waxout had jammed the door lock. They put a bunch of bell captains out to watch all the exits for Waxout. No show. Then Simon called us and we had a car here inside of two minutes. I think we've got Clifford Waxout in the building."

"Okay," the Hunt Leader said briskly, "we start with the empty rooms, then the linen closets, the banquet rooms, ballrooms, the johns. We start low and work our way up to the penthouse. How do we stand on elevators and fire stairs?"

"Six elevators, three in a bank, one bank in the south corridor, one bank in the north. Two fire stairs going all the way."

"Put a man in each elevator. Put two men in each stairway. I don't like the smell of this one. I don't like all this *America's Americans* paperwork thrown around here with all the skull-and-crossbones comics. Maybe we got a real screwball on our hands. And that dame worries me. Suicide pills and FBI Goon Squad. That's Commie talk. Let's swamp the guy Waxout before he knows what hit him."

"Yes, sir." The Sergeant marched briskly to the door, passed a quick assignment to the two uniformed cops in the corridor, then disappeared.

"What...what are you doing in my bag?" dear old Dr. Glover

was heard to inquire of me. The medical man had continued his meddling with Scott Valboa's stupor and had the lad rolling his head and mumbling. Buried in the incoherent strangled sounds stumbling from Scott's throat, the trained ear—there was but one in the room—detected the odious name, "Waxout" roaming on the lad's blunted tongue. Obviously the boy required rest, massive rest.

"It's all right, Doctor," I soothed Glover. "I've found it." I withdrew a hypodermic from the doctor's bag and proceeded to load it with Nembutal.

"May I ask what you intend doing with that?" sayeth Dr. Glover, chuckling and glancing patiently to the police lieutenant and hotel managers. "It may have escaped your attention, young man," Dr. Glover said to me totally condescending, "but I am endeavoring to produce in this patient exactly the opposite response from that which Nembutal will produce. Why don't you just roll your stretcher in here and let me attend to the doctoring?"

"Sorry, Doctor," I said stiffly, "but I cannot stand by and watch you murder the young man. Oh, we've heard about you, Dr. Glover. We get most of your botched up cases down in the emergency ward. 'Glover's Goofs' they're called. Usually it's too late. That little blond-haired girl last month. Even as her heart stopped she had that same bittersweet smile. I've...I've never forgotten her."

Scott Valboa's eyes popped open.

"What's your name?" Dr. Glover screeched at me, through white lips.

"Scott Valboa," the well-disciplined lad on the bed replied.

"What hospital are you from?" the furious doctor continued. "I'll have libel charges against you and your hospital before the night is out!"

"There, there, lad," I said soothingly to Scott. "I'll take care of you." I grabbed his arm and thumbed a vein toward the surface.

"Wait a minute now, wait a minute," the police lieutenant said walking toward the bed. "Before you pump that stuff into his arm let's find out who the doctor is here." The lieutenant had forgotten long ago that there are people in this world who do not listen to police lieutenants. He was still advancing on the bed when I slipped the hollow needle into Scott's arm and shot him six cc's of sleepy time. It would be noon of the next day before young Valboa took again to linking the name Clifford Waxout to the White House recital. Ah, lad, it will be ancient news by then.

"Damn it! I told you to lay off," the lieutenant grunted as he grabbed my arm and expertly spun me away from the bed. I found myself tangled with a chair next to the night table and, just as expertly, tripped over the legs of same breaking a rung. My clumsiness was of such proportions that I staggered on top of the lieutenant who was bending over Scott. Do not tred on me, you gold-badged buffoon.

The impatient lieutenant cursed and pushed me into the center of the room. It is probable that his invective would have been ladled with a heavier hand had he recognized that the hypodermic still in my grasp was somewhat lighter than it had been when I fell on him. Sweet dreams, Lieutenant.

The muscling about with the law was well in keeping with a basic ground rule of the firm of Mandrell Limited but it did however carry its own toll. At some point in the wrestling match Dr. Glover had seen a familiar landmark. "Why, why, that's my gown you have on," he cried. "It has my name on it."

"You're damn right it's yours, Doctor," I snarled. "You left it stuffed in the incision. The little blond-haired girl I mentioned."

"What hospital are you from?" he wailed and turned to the lieutenant for succor.

The lieutenant was blinking and rubbing his face. He put a hand out to the wall.

"You're under arrest, you butcher!" I shouted at Dr. Glover. "You'll never pull another mass murder in this city. Officer! Officer!" I called to a uniformed idiot who was coping with the wide-eyed, eavesdropping crowd at the open door.

The cop pushed against the chest of a black bellhop and turned to look into the room. "Yeah? What do you want done, Lieutenant? You want I should—"

The lieutenant, demonstrating an uncanny talent for timing, chose that moment to crumple slowly to the rug, overturning a floor lamp on the way down.

"What was in those pills you gave the lieutenant?" I screamed at Dr. Glover. "They smelled like bitter almonds."

"You little son of a bitch," the cop from the corridor snarled and advanced toward Glover.

"Just a minute, officer," the crew-cut manager said indignantly, sensing some impending issue of injustice. "Dr. Glover is the house physician. It wasn't he who gave anything to anybody—"

"So you're in on it too, are you?" I hissed. "You and your Russian accent. Line them up against the wall, Officer," I said from the doorway. "I'll get some of your fellow tribesmen to help you."

"Wait a minute," the cop said, reaching for his dreadful gun.

"I can't," I cried. "My ambulance is double parked downstairs." I bulled my way through the ring of nosey-bodies in the corridor, positioning their carcasses between the police artillery and me. "Out of my way," I grinned into my mask. "Haven't you ever seen bubonic plague before? We'll have to burn the body."

I grabbed the door of the fire exit and pulled it open. Myself and a huffing cop who had just come running up the stairs collided in the doorway. He had been in the act of lunging at the fire door. The sudden opening of the portal left him no target for his forward progress other than my frail self. I was driven backwards into the hostile corridor. Speaking of displays of uncanny timing, the god damn D.C. Police Department was riddled with the curse.

The shocked bull and I piled upon the corridor carpet in an ungainly demonstration of impromptu acrobatics. I, of course, was first to my feet but the brutish encounter had cost me a portion of my shield. My hot surgical mask had been torn from my face by the sharp edge of the copper's badge. (There, my dear readers, for those of you who chomp upon grotesque portents and insidious omens, there is a choice chunk of diseased flesh.)

"That's him! That's him! That's Clifford Waxout!" cried a voice in the vicinity of room 1616.

I took one quick glance as I darted again into the fire exit. Dr. Glover was at the doorway of my old room, my bus-station room, pointing a vindictive finger at me. Beside him stood the baffled cop, his revolver, guided my indecision, rearing its brute mouth in my direction.

I threw the fire stair door wide so that the cop coming up from the carpet should see me plunge on to the "down" flight of stairs. As soon as the door swung back to its frame I, of course, reversed my flight and sprung like a great silent rodent for the "up" stairs. I was past the 17th floor landing and on my way to the 18th before the sounds of the two cops and their thrilled volunteers spilled onto the 16th landing.

I exited quietly on the 18th floor. The first door I knocked on produced a muffled, "Just a minute." I fled to the next corridor. There was no response from beyond the portal of 1829. I communicated with the lock; my interpreter a slender bit of steel from the lining of my notecase. I was granted asylum.

By gad but the hounds were pressing in earnest. Cops in the elevators. Cops in the stairwells. And in 15 minutes Consuela would be waiting for me in the White House limousine at the basement carport.

You miserable, salivating hyena! Already you have stolen from me my hour of bliss, my 60 sweet minutes that were to have been devoted to rifling the plumage of the eye-stopping nightingale. Now, you swine, you incompetent jackasses with your diluted egos, now you dare tamper with Mandrell Limited's reputation for performance, our operational procedures—my income!

Lock Augustus Mandrell in your rat's nest hotel, will you? Bah!

I scooped up the telephone in my 18th floor sanctuary and asked for the desk. The voice of the clerk who answered oozed with efficient normalcy, a gooey sound; manhunt in progress in our hotel? Heavens no.

"Hey this is Arnie Heterosexual," I said, slurring the name. "I'm in 1828 and I want to get something straight. There's a Mr. Waxout here at my door who claims you told him to double up with me."

"You say you're in room 1828, Mr...er..?" He was thumbing through cards.

"Yeah, 1828. Now look, this guy Waxout has a funny look in his eye. He—Hey! Hey let go 'a the phone! Let go, you son of a bitch..." I swung the speaking end of the receiver against a water glass shattering same. I then dropped the instrument on the table where it recorded for the desk clerk not only the clatter of its impact on broken glass but also the grotesque strangulation gasps emitting from my throat. How's that for normalcy, my friend?

It appeared probable that several law enforcers would visit room 1828 shortly, a room just down the corridor. I high-tailed myself to the 19th floor.

On the 19th floor I planned to mingle with several of my fellow guests. The life of the harried fugitive is, in truth, a lonely life. My formal attire was hardly the costume to impress these residents of the posh 19th floor; the spacing of their entry doors alone indicated the rooms beyond be at least twice the size of the lower income quarters on the other floors. Yet to impress the 19th floor gentry was my intention. One likes to be noticed.

Accordingly, I removed from the wall a fire axe, the head of which was painted red but configured still along the clean utilitarian line of such insistent instruments. Next to the axe mount was a reel of fire hose. Pity to break up the set. I grabbed the nozzle.

With the axe in one hand and the flat ominous rubber tube trailing after me I roamed the corridor tapping discreetly on closed doors.

The door to 1920 was opened by a middle-aged chap holding a copy of *Time Magazine* in his hand. "Great Scott!" I greeted him, "haven't you evacuated yet? Didn't—"

Two other doors in my wake opened. "My God," I cried going pale (child's play.) "What are all you people doing here? Don't you know the complete 16th floor is ablaze? We thought the building was empty. Didn't you get the phone call?"

I started running. "Are there any others?" I called, now close to panic and leaving clean broken-wood nicks where I pounded on doors with my axe. "My God, are there any children?"

Doors located forward of my zigzag line of progress were now being opened without the urging of my long-handled door knocker. The hubbub of the corridor voices had drawn forth the slightly indignant residents. Actually I had to restrain my articulate axe in mid-flight on one occasion as the door toward which it flew was opened abruptly by a large Italian-looking gentleman wearing only shoes, socks, a healthy moustache, and a thick-belted truss. He watched silently as I sped on.

The hose I'd been towing reached the extreme of its extension and a rather frightening alarm bell clanged joylessly in the corridors, evidently actuated by the pull of the mounted end of the hose against its stop. The dozen or so residents who were already disgorging from their apartments with leaking suitcases momentarily froze in their tracks. Then the ladies of their ranks, robe-clad for the most part, attempted to bury the alarm bell under a vocal parasol of screams. The stream of suitcase-carrying refugees scurrying for the fire stairs accelerated the tempo of their flight. One can only hope that their disorganized downward travel will not impede the activities of the policemen stationed in the stairwells.

This whole unsightly commotion was in progress in the south corridor of the 19th floor. How are the folks in the north corridor reacting to the holocaust, Augustus? I galloped along the connecting east hallway where a few folks were peering from their doors.

The clamor from the south had not penetrated the insulated walls of the north. Again I pulled the fire hose from its reel and advanced along the carpeted tunnel of complacency. A vigorous life, this fire fighting. This time however I cranked open the wall valve in order to provide nourishment for my rubber snake. The pile-driving stream of water striking the apartment doors did not have the authoritative heft of the fire axe but I felt the sudden staccatic rattling of the complete door in its frame would surely ignite the curiosity of the guests beyond those doors. Ah, yes. At a few doors to my rear I heard the muffled question, "Who is there?" I threw the hose nozzle from me and permitted my animated snake to writhe and whiplash about on the carpeting; a gushing, dancing orator capable of delivering his own sermon.

It was time to visit the 20th floor.

As you no doubt have realized the Clifford Waxout disguise I wore, while surely a confectionary masterpiece, was not in the least wieldy. This consideration, plus an unhappy fact that the end result of my cosmetic labors did indeed leave me with the face of Mr. Waxout, made the Waxout disguise one of the less endearing of the masks that I have assembled during my years with Mandrell Limited.

(Which brings to mind: Someday I must paw through the concept of fathering a son who will inherit the firm, a fine prosperous business for an energetic young man. Ah, Consuela, with that fire trapped in your thighs, perhaps our union would have produced... Incidentally, while we are probing this issue of my issue, I wish to lay to rest those unkind rumors that have prevailed in the British Isles since Mrs. Thomas Roche (nee Hope Cornflower) bore her child just six months following her flamboyant wedding at the Bullrusher Estate. You do recall the affair do you not, my friends: The Bullrusher Commission? That delightful Italian dressmaker, Senor Orlando with his passion for m'lady's internal dimensions? Colorful chap. Anyway, the fact that Hope Cornflower was found nude and incoherent, and miraculously unscarred from the boating accident, on the shores of Bemont Lake approximately nine months prior to the birth of her child is hardly justification to question her account of the events that took place on the lake that evening. She has stated officially that she was taken to the gates of Heaven by a certain young English officer, a Lieutenant Dan Gregg, and, while awaiting the arrival of the guardian of that portal, she engaged in certain rites designed to ensure a residency of tranquility and contemplation in the Great Beyond. To insist on a description from the lady of those rites is, I feel, unwarranted trespassing into the details of the Lord's passport regulations. I'm certain that any of you have been justifiably spellbound by the description of the whole ruddy business appearing in The American Mistress Commission—yes, I still draw a few pounds in royalties now and again—will agree with me. Personally I pay no heed to the speculative rumors and have not done so ever since the day of the birth of Tom and Hope Roche's child. Young Miss Rachel Cornflower, despite the somewhat rebellious nature that has caused her to insist on using her mother's maiden name, is doing quite well in her schooling, I am told.)

But back to the 20th floor of my Washington, D.C. prison. The Clifford Waxout disguise, as I have indicated, was not one of your pop-on pop-off facades. Since I had yet before me in the evening a labor that required the Waxout face I could hardly discard the bits and pieces nor the garments which supplemented the role despite the fact that every cop in the joint was aware that the quarry was a distinguished looking, baldheaded chap dressed in formal attire. I was forced to retain the costume but not necessarily all of it, at least not all of it during my venture on the 20th floor. I removed my trousers.

Thus arrayed: Faithful fire axe in one hand, trousers rolled under one arm, I went tap tap tapping at many doors on the 20th floor. As ever, I wore no shorts.

To each of the kindly residents who opened their door to me I said, "My name is Clifford Waxout. Does my wife chance to be here?" I wiggled my axe and smiled knowingly.

Many of the doors, I am forced to report, were slammed in my face. American hospitality, old man? Non-existent.

A few gentlemen did step forth from their rooms and follow me in the corridor commenting gallantly on their displeasure at having their wives, who had answered my knock, exposed to my "advertisement," as one gentleman put it. These hearties, though, were discouraged from registering anything more abusive than a verbal complaint since my habit, as I moved from door to door, was to swish the axe around broadsword fashion. For the most part the reaction at the various portals was a quick gasp by the door opener (no, no, sir, I am not the bragging sort) followed by a headlong rush to the telephone.

Eventually, as I was displaying my axe work in the west corridor I heard a babble of strenuous voices in my wake in the north corridor and the clang of opening elevator doors. The blue insect herd had invaded the 20th floor. My entourage, sensing the arrival of sympathetic ears, ran away from me toward the sound. Unfaithful blabbermouths.

I slipped into a room from which there had been no response and picked up the telephone. There was a full minute's wait before connection to the desk was given life. In the corridor outside my room unhealthy feet pounded the carpet first in one direction then the other.

The desk answered. "Yeah? What now?"

Ah, my son, I suspect you are on foreign assignment. "This is Mr. Robert Root in room 2106," I said. "I wish to issue a formal complaint with the management. Whom should I speak to?"

"What's the beef?" the bored voice inquired.

"Well, there's this- well he's hardly a gentleman, a man anyway, there's little doubt of that, which is walking in our corridor with a fire axe and no trousers on. Now my wife who—"

"You're on the 21st floor?" he said, the boredom shattered. He broke away from the mouthpiece to shout to somebody at his end. "Tell the damn nitwits there is no fire. Tell them to go back up to their rooms. Hello? Hello?"

"I'm still here," I answered. "Yes, this is the 21st floor. What's that about a fire? Is the hotel on fire?"

"No, no, no fire, pal. The 21st floor is the top floor isn't it?"

"Yes, I believe so. Nothing above me but the roof. And the penthouse of course."

"Good! That means we got him. Which corridor is he in?" To someone at his end of the connection he whispered, "Ed, get your sharpshooters onto the roof of the Navsec building across the street."

"Just a minute, I'll ask my wife," I said. "Which corridor is he in, dear? She's gone out for another look." I let the fish wiggle for a few seconds. "Hello? My wife says the man just went up the stairs toward the penthouse—No, no, dear, don't go out there again... Josephine...!"

I broke the telephone connection with my finger. I released the button and again asked the operator for the desk. "And please hurry," I pleaded, in a worried soprano voice. While I held the telephone with my jaw I slipped my trousers on. Sorry, Josephine.

A different voice answered at the desk phone. It sounded like that of the clerk I'd spoken to earlier regarding the Mr. Waxout who claimed he was to double up with me. A considerable portion of the clerk's composure had been drained by the events swirling about the front desk. Possibly you are not quite ready for big time hotel management, my son.

In the background at his end of the line there was an audible and invigorating volume of baffled shouting. This sobering sound surrounded and occasionally overwhelmed one emotional voice that kept repeating: "Please, please, ladies and gentlemen, go back to your rooms..."

"This is Miss Martin in 1816," I told the clerk. "These two policemen are here in my room and—"

"Yes, yes, Miss Martin, we know. I'm terribly sorry but we are searching all the rooms on the 18th floor. You see—"

"I didn't mind that," I interrupted with girlish anger. "I let them search the room. But I see no reason why it has to go further, why they have to search me. I'm standing here like a fool in my undies and I refuse to take off another stitch." I slapped my face and snapped, "Get your hands away from me, you beast! And stop taking off your clothes!"

To the, presumably engrossed chap at the desk I cried, "Will you tell whoever is in charge of these...these animals...let go of me! Get your hand out of there!" My scream contained that touching primordial echo that tends to curl one's hair.

I rapped the receiver against the wall several times then held it at arm's length. The clerk's hysterical "Miss Martin? Miss Martin?" was still coming over the line. I brought the mouthpiece a bit closer and grunted, "Dat's it Bruno. Keep dem pretty legs spread out like dat. Hot damn, dis is gonna be more fun than dem two twelve-year-olds down the hall." My finger quietly broke the connection. We got a he-man's work going on up here buddy, we don't need no outsiders.

On the next call I did not bother asking for the desk. I imparted to the operator alone the rather titillating intelligence that a man with no trousers was standing on the edge of the hotel roof waving what appeared to be a fire axe at the moon and screaming, "I'm coming up there and cut your ass in half!" The lady gasped and the line immediately went dead.

I looked out the window of my 20th floor nest and observed that the room I wished to visit was located two doors away. I, incidentally, saw no man on the roof edge. One hopes he didn't...

The connecting back-to-back doors to the next room fell before my pick, rather to the surprise of the middle-aged couple who lived therein and who were, at the moment of intrusion, solemnly dressing for dinner.

"Don't worry folks," I said smiling at them. "The boa constrictor got loose from the kitchen again. He's slithering up the outside wall of the building. But we'll get him. We always do." The explanation was accompanied by an adroit wiggling of the fire axe, my obvious mastery of the weapon inducing, I'm certain, their full confidence.

The couple endured the invasion with considerable pluck. The man cleared his throat a few times while I was opening the doors to the next room but said nothing. The woman, after a quarter of a minute or so, asked, "What...what is a boa constrictor, Edward?"

Edward's reply was lost to me forever behind the doors which I locked as I passed into the next room. I did, however, hear him lift the telephone. This new room I at first took to be unoccupied. Then the waves of fetid alcoholic air emanating from the area of the bed washed upon my nostrils. In a few seconds I was able to make out the aromatic figure sprawled across the bed. It was a lady of some 40 summers whose retirement that evening had evidently been abrupt. She had managed to get out of her dress and one shoe and to detach the garters holding her nylons to her black girdle. Then the excesses of her evening's reverie had taken their revenge. She was on her back, her thin, rather pretty arms flung outward; not a care in the world, until hangover time.

Alas, you don't think, Augustus, that this comely lass could possibly be the harried Miss Martin? Those brass-buttoned brutes had to ply her with booze in order to have their way with her. No, no, I think not. Miss Martin resides on the 18th floor. Besides, as I recall, Miss Martin is a younger woman. Well, ladies residing in big cities should always be prepared, or so I have heard. I opened the maid's hand and inserted therein the handle of my faithful fire axe. The fingers tightened about the wooden shaft and the lady appeared to smile slightly. Woe be to any incautious rapist who invades this boudoir, eh my dear?

Well, now, what say a quick review of the travail that has overtaken the noble hostellery? We have those poor routed folk on the 19th floor fleeing the fire. Then we have the shocked residents of the 20th and 21st floors submitting updated itineraries on the travels of the semi-nude Clifford Waxout and his keen-edged plaything. The assault on Miss Martin reported on the 18th, surely it has not failed to elicit some degree of indignation. And lastly, the possible untidy conclusion to the chase, as indicated by Mr. Waxout's acrobatics on the roof-edge, must have fluttered an insurance-oriented heart or two; all those innocent up-turned faces on the sidewalks below.

I would say that the D.C. Police Department could hardly be faulted for lack of evidence had they concluded that success was to be enjoyed only if large numbers of blue-suited minions were dispatched to the upper floors of the hotel. Certainly there was little reason to maintain dense surveillance of any floor below the 18th. Time, I'd say, for the discreet man to seek the shelter of some floor in that unpatrolled vacuum.

Ah, but not by trespassing the corridors. There one might encounter a copper who had yet to be advised regarding the latest point of attack, the roof.

I eased open the French doors and reconnoitered the balcony which abutted the apartment of the alcoholic sleeping beauty. The balcony was one of a vertical row of such tasteful platforms, which ran up the side of the building, each attached to the exterior of one of the hotel's choicer rooms. In the cool distance one could see the lighted slab sides of the Washington Monument. And that glow in mid-town there, Augustus, is that not the residence of that chap you have labored so mightily to enjoin in adventure? Yes, indeed, the President's White House.

It had been the balcony adornment that had drawn me to this particular room. When normal human exits and entrances are barred to the willful man you may find that he will revert to the pathways of his ancestors. One simply climbs over the edge of the protective rail, lowers oneself, hangs for a moment with a slight inward swing of the body, releases one's grip, and thump! Why then one is no longer on the 20th floor but on the 19th. Chap named Newton has some rather fascinating formulas regarding the whole ruddy process.

The room located off the balcony on the 19th floor was deserted but the lights were on and the door to the corridor was open. Evidently the lodgings of one of those poor wretches driven from his hearth by the flames of the holocaust.

A policeman lumbered past the open corridor door. The idiot was carrying his pistol in his hand. Over the wall, Augustus.

Three gentlemen seated in the room on the 18th floor drinking cocktails lifted their heads and looked at each other as though they had heard some portion of the noise I generated landing on their balcony. I was on my way to the 17th floor before any bestirred himself to investigate.

The room on the 17th floor appeared to be unoccupied. I pried my way through the French doors and picked up the telephone. Time to report in. My old friend, the flustered clerk, eventually came on the line. You continue to patrol the breach despite the reports of chaos in the heavens above your head, do you, old man? Stout chap.

"I say, this is Mr. Ill Tidings in 1708," I rattled off, emphasizing the room number. "Hate to bother you but I'm afraid it's out of control."

"Out...out of control?"

"Yes, thought I could put it out by myself. Kept stomping on it, threw some blankets on it and the like but-ha, ha,- the blankets just went up too."

"The what, the what?" he pleaded. "Not...not a fire?" he whispered.

"Afraid so. The draperies—lovely material—went up rather quickly. I tried to save them, smother them with the mattress, you know, but -ha, ha,- now the mattress is on fire and has fallen in front of the lavatory door. The flames are rather well underway actually. I'm somewhat reluctant to lay hold of the mattress even though it is causing the lavatory door to ignite."

"That's 1708, right? Okay, now listen. I'll get the fire department. You pack your clothes and get out of the room. And—this is important—make sure you close the door to the room, the corridor door. Do you understand?"

"Yes, of course. But what about my wife?"

"Your wife?"

"Yes. Poor dear, she's in the lavatory bathing and, well we've been together for a number of years now—"

"We'll be right up," he screamed.

"Another thing –" I started to say.

"Just a minute," he interrupted. "Mr. Maxwell!" he called to someone. "Mr. Maxwell, there's a real one in 1708...yes, a real one of *those*." To me, the trembling voice said, "Don't worry 1708, members of the staff are on their way."

"I do wish they'd hurry," I said, my own voice losing a bit of its aplomb. "That thing is most of the way in the window now."

"Thing?"

"The boa constrictor."

The impact of his telephone on the marble-topped front desk jarred in my ear. Speaking of things anthropological, Augustus, I'd say it was time for you to demonstrate once more your inheritance from your simian forebears. Over the rail to the 16th, to the floor of your former home.

The room off the balcony on the 16th level was rather a large living room in which a celebration of considerable alcoholic embellishment was in progress. Two smaller rooms, one to each side, had been opened to provide the revelers increased acreage for their boisterous swilling. The French doors were open to permit the slight breeze from the Potomac River access to the faded gray cigarette smoke that was seeking panicked escape from recirculation in the polluted sacks of some thirty pairs of lungs within the rooms.

I adjusted my dress suit and was about to advance into the center of the festivities. Then a shoe scraped on the cement off in the dark corner of the balcony. A young couple stood there staring at me, the girl pushing her hair back into place.

I shrugged to them and remarked, "Aw, the guy upstairs doesn't have any ice cubes either. I'll try across the hall." I withdrew into the room.

An angry looking young man shouldered his way to me and asked, "Who were you talking to out there?" He moved on toward the French doors without waiting for my reply. "Bernice, are you out there?" he said, announcing the advance of his forces. Questionable tactics, Sgt. Major, highly questionable.

The incident, which went almost unnoticed in the general welter of laughter and conversation, did draw several inquiring eyes toward the balcony. Once the young man disappeared in the gloom, these eyes shifted and landed ungentle on myself. My passage to the corridor door would contain, I felt, considerable occasion for embarrassing challenge. I needed allies in this room of strangers. And to accumulate allies one is well advised to establish a common enemy.

I threw off my outer shell of fine-tooled aplomb and with a surprised smile I waved toward the other side of the room and called, "Annie! Annie, you little dickens..." I bungled my way forward, carefully directing my progress around the cocktail-holding human barriers toward a certain target, a bearded folk singer. He was seated on the rug with his guitar, his back against the potable bar deliberately blocking a portion of the most highly traveled roadway in the room with a fierce facial expression of the determinedly just.

I timed my arrival in his vicinity to coincide with his act of crushing out his cigarette in a small glass ashtray at his side. The clumsy planting of my foot on his paw, his tool of multiple musical sins, could not have been more accidental. There was considerable activity then as several ladies in delightfully low-cut gowns and myself aided the young man to the rear of the bar and attempted to dislodge the shards of glass from his hand. The hired bartender with the name of "Walter S." embroidered on his white jacket demonstrated a rather shocking lack of humanitarianism when he noted that several times I misdirected the folk singer's leaking wound over the tray of pre-cut lemon peels, cherries, olives, and onions.

"Christ, watch out with the dripping blood there, Buddy," he instructed me. Possibly he feared his exotic fluid added to his cocktail trimmings would find flavor with the guests and create a demand the bar would be hard pressed to resupply. The guests might then turn one upon the other in an effort to satisfy their new appetite. And should the whole thing receive coverage in the Bartender's News, with Walter S.'s name linked to the latest craze in bars throughout the land...

Obviously Walter S. was reluctant to shoulder responsibilities of celebrity status. He eased me out of the makeshift operating room with an adroit shove of his hip, causing me to stumble backwards and step on the young musician's guitar. That chord, with its background accompaniment of splintering varnished wood, I don't recall having heard before.

At this point the allies I spoke of came forward to enfold me in their cause. These were four staggering gentlemen with appropriately thinning hair and rotund midriffs who had been gathered in arm-linked conspiracy behind one of the sofas. In this upholstered redoubt they had been attempting to summon the ghost of their university days by engaging in a vocal entreaty to the New England mutton god: Ba-ba-baaah.

The staggering quartet surrounded me and spoke grandly of my victory in my single-handed combat with musical dark knight from that mysterious land: Younger Generation. Here was the Palace Guard I needed in the hostile kingdom. No one dared invade our ranks to issue bureaucratic questions regarding my credentials; my printed invitation, for instance.

I was released by my bleary juveniles only after I issued solemn assurance that I would return momentarily from my room down the hall with my mandolin. The door to the corridor was opened for me by a lovely woman in her thirties, a blonde with an intricate hair-do and the bluest eyes I have ever seen. She sped me on my way with a cheerful, "And don't bother to come back. You freeloading son of a bitch." The hostess, I believe.

At last, the corridor of the 16th floor. Now, an opportunity to assess the effectiveness of my deployment of the blue-coated enemy. The south corridor was empty except for a young man waiting for the elevator. I walked past my old room, 1616. The door had been reinstalled on the defiled cubicle. What have you buried therein, you fiends, that you must seal the tomb? I would presume that you summoned the required manpower to remove the trench coat clad Scott Valboa. In his slumbering state, the 6 cc's of Nembutal coursing in his bloodstream, he could hardly have been expected to sign a registration card.

With a handkerchief to my nostrils I watched the young man standing by the elevator, watched for his reaction as the car dropped from the upper floors and then halted to take him aboard. The doors opened and the lad ambled into the car. There was no pause of the type one might exhibit if confronted by an elevator full of coppers. As the door slid toward its closed position I strode briskly by the opening, my frantic eye cornering for an inventory of the elevator's uniformed population. Not a blue suit in sight!

I spun and knifed through the diminishing opening. My forward momentum carried me into abrupt contact with the young idiot who had unaccountably stopped just inside the door. Our collision threw him to the rear of the car where he banged up against a pert damsel of some twenty summers, the only other passenger. The lad's clumsy, arm-flailing encounter with the maid was of somewhat greater intensity than might be expected. I mean he appeared to be constructed along the wiry, athletic lines of a good rugby forward. Ah, the additional layers of leather in the heels of your shoes, my boy, there is the source of the misinformation fed to your stability center. The American preoccupation with being "taller than she is." My observation leads me to believe that it is the American ladies who insist on this artificial sense of domination; for what reason, I'm certain they shall never reveal.

Ah well, lad, it matters not the rationale, you are certainly properly shod for our brief downward encounter...elevator shoes. The young buffoon spent the entire ride apologizing to the maid, in particular addressing the clutch of violets that had dislodged from her dress during their abrupt introduction. The lass tended to ignore him for the duration of our descent past the 15th and 14th floors, preferring instead to glare at me. But biology happily has been with us forever, anger comes and goes. Eventually the young maid encouraged the young man to consider reattaching her corsage with his own two hands. Initially his faint-hearted fingers attempted to anchor the violets in the vicinity of her clavicle. The young miss, feigning cute impatience, sweetly drew the bumbling fingers down to the correct point of installation, the area just above the enchanting thrust of anatomy he had been painfully avoiding. The thoroughly rattled boob dropped the corsage again. My God, how do we men ever survive?

I spared the juveniles but cursory attention. I was engaged in electronic combat with the innards of the elevator control box. I had the panel swung open and used the maintenance pushbutton to encourage the docile wires to reject all signals received from any floor located between the 16th floor and the basement. The elevator thus dropped giddily without a stop to the hotel's underground garage; the row of lighted numbers above the door popping on and off like a string of firecrackers as the proud car, for one joyous trip, was free to plunge downward past all those pipsqueak doorways that were forever reigning in the metal mustang. Were some statistician chap to look into the event, I'm certain he would conclude that a new world record for the 17th floor elevator drop was established that day.

The children behind me, enmeshed in their own vale of tears, noted not that their chosen exit, the hotel lobby, had been bypassed. Their program of floral arrangement was still in progress as I closed the elevator control box, pressed the lobby button, and stepped out of the car as the door slid closed. And I stepped into ruddy bedlam!

The underground parking area was awash in a frightful uproar. Cursing firemen were attempting to maneuver two red and chrome behemoths in the narrow lanes available in the sea of dwarf vehicles belonging to the hotel guests. Revolving yellow lights painted the drab cement walls with shifting color, frightening spiders from ancient webs. Clanging bells engaged in mortal combat with the deep roar of the fire-truck diesel engines as the drivers fought to inch their pulsating chargers past the protruding bumpers of long Cadillacs and Lincolns. Yellow-slickered firemen dragged flat hoses over the roofs of parked cars to God only knows where. Majestic men in polished helmets shouted into battery-operated bullhorns, providing frustrated guidance to the anonymous ant hoard deploying the serpent hoses. Absolutely chaotic beauty!

I ran, ran, ran, skipping over hoses, dodging the helmeted generals, ignoring those who held up leveled fingers intended to redirect my travel. There remained but one short flight of stairs and the limousine port one floor above, between brilliant escape and me!

A correction. There remained in my path one short flight of stairs and one bear-tempered matron. As I pounded up the cement steps, there loomed on the landing above me the unkempt bulk of Polly Culver, our baffled visitor from Portland, Oregon. She had been in the act of descending this same set of stairs, possibly also in flight. The unsavory clutches of Mr. Simon, the hotel detective, had failed to enchant her. Although, to judge by the torn fabric of her outer garments, I would guess that the gentleman had not lacked in energetic ardor.

Polly's formidable eye had hardly been dimmed by her Washington adventure. The orbs glinted with tapped venom as she recognized the well-dressed gentleman who paused on the staircase five steps below her.

"That's it, Mr. Waxout, run and keep on running," she screeched. "You will be running from now on. I'll see to that."

"My dear Polly, are you changing hotels? A wise move. The din in this place is unbelievable. If you want a suggestion—"

"I've got friends on *America's Americans* Central Committee, Mr. Waxout," she continued with her own preoccupation. "And I know enough about the ones who are not friends, like Martin Crossfox, to keep them in line. Do you know who'll be the new Director of Northwest, Mr. Waxout? They'll elect me! You idiot, you wouldn't have lasted a week without me anyway. I've always been the real director."

"I say, is that someone paging me?" I said and moved upwards. As I dodged around her I patted her bare shoulder where her dress had been torn. "Lovely gown my dear, but a bit too West Coast for Washington, if you don't mind my saying." I lunged for the door to the outer grounds.

"You're finished in AA, Clifford," she screamed after me. "What you need is a psychiatrist. Clifford...Clifford are you listening to me?"

No, my dear, I cannot honestly say that I am.

I moved quickly across the small lawn maintained by the hotel and around the corner of the tall building. I was forced to progress within the deeper shadows close to the shrubbery for on the sidewalks were twenty or so ladies, gentlemen, and a sprinkling of urchins dressed in robes and standing beside suitcases. They appeared to be in need of a leader and for the most part gazed upward on the face of the building as though this mentor were due to arrive at any moment via parachute or possibly snow sled. I avoided their eyes for I felt that I could provide them no more guidance than those fire-hose sermons I had already preached on the 19th floor.

The carport! There stood the White House Cadillac. The vehicle was distinguishable from the other majestic limousines parked in regal line by its lack of exterior bright work; a sadly unfrocked machine, de-chromed to an austere virility thought to be in keeping with its mission. When will the Americans ever learn?

Consuela DiMartino, her exquisite shoulders protruding from a lavender gown, was seated in the back of the auto. She evidently spied me for the uniformed chauffer left his post and hurried to open the door.

"My goodness, Clifford, I'd begun to think you weren't coming."

"My sweet diva, I wouldn't miss it for the world. I've been looking forward to it for such a long time."

The chauffer closed the padded door.

The pre-concert intermesh of the peasants at the White House presented an interesting sociological exhibit. Those who feel the Americans are a people removed from royalist behavior in their heralded republic should stand in a White House reception room someday and gage the fierce undercurrent of anticipation in force preceding the arrival of the President and the First Lady. About the only marked difference I could detect, as compared with those occasions when I and other guests awaited the arrival of the born sovereign of some kingdom or other, relates to the fact that at the White House you must expect, with rare exception, to be presented to a new face every four or eight years.

On the surface, the twitter of conversation overheard by the lovely Diva and myself concerned the lives of those engaged in the twittering. But there were great flapping wings in motion just beneath the conversational crust, each person's awareness of just which house he stood in and just who was to enter through yon portal at any moment now.

"I've been trying to count," Consuela whispered to me, her hot breath drawing blood to my ear, "but I keep losing track. I'm sure there must be 76 guests."

"Yes, I don't suppose Old 76 has departed from his numerical limitation even for you, my lovely." My eyes held hers for a second and then, almost out of control, slid down over her wet lips, over the slender neck that contained the magic voice, and finally arrived in a soft, feather landing on the rounded, mouth-watering portions of her breasts that escaped the cruel cover of her dress.

"Oh, Clifford, don't," her whisper pleaded. "I won't remember a word of my aria. Oh, God, how I wish these two hours were over."

Slowly I brought a cold, mailed fist to my head to gather my senses and curl hard, steel fingers around those witless emotions for which discipline is a least consideration. I tore my eyes from the maiden, from the parts of her that gnawed at my resolve, but I was not quick enough to slam the door on my throat. The pain-drenched word, "Consuela..." escaped my mouth and ran into her outstretched arms.

I shook my head and said, "Ah, yes, my dear, our President's obsession with the significance of the number 76 is certainly worthy of examination by a charitable psychiatrist."

My remark evidently seeped out of our clutch of isolation. Then, I should have anticipated that I could not hold the world-famous songbird cemented to my wants alone in that room of milling antidote-oriented professionals. A matron shrouded in the finest efforts of that season's preferred New York couturier, recognized the opening and lunged with alert and vocal stiletto.

"Oh, Miss DiMartino, you wouldn't believe, I mean you are out of the country so much with your concert tours, you wouldn't believe how the President is absorbed...absolutely obsessed...with this 76 thing. 76 suits in his closet, 76 personal aids in the White House, 76 push-ups every morning, 76 brands of beer in his refrigerator, 76 this, 76 that. My husband, Robert Lloyd, he's the Lloyd of Beushausen, Lloyd, Dechenbaugh and Clayton; the vehicular remerchandizing people? Robert says the President even believes..." She paused, realizing she had us trapped in the net of civilized politeness, and casually rolled her medicated eyes to our left and right.

"Robert believes the President is even convinced he will die, er, expire, at age 76. Can you believe that?"

Ah, my brash lady, perhaps the gentleman will reevaluate his timetable once this evening has, er, *expired.*

A Negro dressed in a diplomatic-gray formal called for our attention in a beautiful English-accented voice. When we had quieted, when the herd had settled down, the black man said, "Ladies and Gentlemen, the President of the United States." I will say that the Americans do that rather well.

Tall double doors were pulled open and in he came; dental smile, gold-rimmed glasses, and the hungry hand outstretched looking for a partner, possibly to test the resilience developed in 76 push-ups every morning.

We, 76 guests fell dutifully into queue along the perimeter of the fine old room and awaited our turn to hear the artificial, "Glad you could make it," from the boss's lips.

Consuela, despite her years on the receiving end of public adulation, was childishly impressed and delighted. The warmth, the precision-cut coziness afloat in the room slowly folded about her senses. I deliberately positioned myself behind her in the perfumed line of people, out of contact with her simmering green eyes. I watched the enchantment of the occasion slowly lure my Diva away from me as the reception line moved inexorably toward my, ah well, target, expresses it as well as any word. Think what you will, but at one point a strange, for me, jealousy laid hold of my caution and I brought myself slowly forward until I made warm contact with what one French critic has identified as, "the most dramatic derriere in opera today." (There appears to be unanimous accord on this particular issue.)

I was rewarded by a momentary backward thrust initiated by the lady. I had succeeded in retrieving her awareness at least to the extent of hearing her moan, "Oh, Clifford..."

Enough, Augustus. Find yourself new avenues of interest. How many secret service goons can you identify in this room, for instance?

As my casual eye surveyed the large portrait-draped room, my ear also opened to the non-DiMartino world. A woman's voice behind me was saying, "The man must be out of his head, trying to promote a movie that way."

"Oh, he claims it's just coincidence but that's ridiculous," answered a tall distinguished looking chap two slots back. A group of two couples were engaged in the conversation. "The title of the movie was, quote, 'Set In Cement', unquote, a year before the police in Louisville found the girl's head in the bus station locker. That's what he says."

"Coincidence, hell." The man nearest me offered. "It's not like 'Steel Around His Neck' was part of the American idiom, an old Ben Franklin axiom. Harry Alucard has made his bucks selling gore on the screen for years. He's from the old horror-equals-boff school of Hollywood. That girl's leg the cops found in the bus station locker in Lancaster, Pennsylvania had the words: STEEL AROUND HIS NECK. Some coincidence!"

"Did you ever see that terrible one where all the pretty dogs died?" The heavy-set lady adjacent to me asked the lady with the distinguished-looking chap. "What was the title of that one, Marvin?" she asked her husband, the Confirmed Doubter.

"Oh, 'The Rabid Mailman' or some such rubbish," the Doubter answered. "I'll tell you they got pretty excited over at the Post Master General's when that one hit the screens. Dogs biting a mailman and up and dying. Not too peachy keen for the Post Office image-wise."

"It's going to be interesting to see what the FBI comes up with," Mr. Distinguished-looking said, "They've got all the parts here in town now: the head from Louisville, the arm and leg from Bridgeport, and the arm and leg from Lancaster. I wonder how locker-rental stock is going?"

"Oh, Howard..." the lady next to Distinguished-looking said. "Anyway, finding out that Hollywood is somehow involved with this girl-in-the-locker thing has certainly lessened the public's interest. It's like seeing a sort of Southern California fungus spreading over the insides of a new toy."

"I'm afraid you're right, my dear," Howard answered. "Down at the Post we've decided to give the story subordinate coverage."

"Ah, the gentlemen of the press are here. Are you ready for the greatest headline of your career, Howard?"

"I still say they should do something about that producer, Harry Alucard," the plump lady wailed. "You do realize what his name spelled backwards is, don't you?"

"They can't do much to him if they can't find him," said her husband, was his name Marvin? "Even the FBI boys can't lay their hands on him. I hear some of the money-boys up in New York are really worried. Harry Alucard has a million dollars worth of publicity going for 'Steel Around His Neck" backed by some heavyweights, but the film ain't 'in the can' yet, as they say. But nobody can find Harry and Alucard is one of those producers who does the whole bit with his pictures: writing, directing, producing, cleaning out the ashtrays."

A youngish man with tight brown hair touched my elbow. "Mr. Clifford Waxout?" he asked politely.

When I nodded the man said, "We'd like to request that you move on to the recital room and take your seat for the performance."

What is this, "we'd"? Who are the "we"? Careful, Augustus.

Consuela had turned to the composed young man. "Will you please explain," she said, prepared to unsheathe her talons. "Mr. Waxout is my guest."

"We are aware of that, Miss DiMartino," the man said with a boyish smile. "It's just that we're a bit behind schedule and we're trying to cut down on the time here in the reception."

"But," Consuela started to say.

I interrupted. "My sweet, it's all right. I understand this timetable dilemma," I lied. "Give them the performance of your life." I kissed her hand, leaving thereon the vivid track of my hot tongue. "Let's go, young man," I said to the polite one.

He escorted me through a door that located me away from that where the President stood. We moved along a varnished corridor where our footsteps were stridently audible. "The Lincoln Room is over this way," he said, opening another door and holding it for me. His tone was cooler but somehow I could not regard him as an immediate menace to my intentions. He appeared too matter-of-factly efficient and his eyes, for instance, failed to monitor the movements of my hands.

As we moved across the carpeted room that would bring us in behind the room where the reception was in progress, I said, "Now that the ladies have gone to their tea, may I ask what this is all about?"

"The President just doesn't want to shake hands with you, Mr. Waxout, that's all."

"And did he chance to mention why?"

"I think you should know why. We didn't have a hell of a lot of time to look you up, but we did the best we could."

"Look me up?"

"Yeah, we did find out quite a bit about you, Jack. You and your *America's Americans*."

"Oh that."

Another carpeted corridor brought us to the recital room. Rows of comfortable chairs with wooden arms and embroidered back rests were arranged facing a one-step high platform at the front of the room upon which stood a black, highly polished piano. I was shown my reserved seat by my grimly disciplined escort. My chair was located six rows back and to the right of where the Chief Executive would be sitting. Not what one might classify as a position of prestige but a location admirably tailored to my ambitions.

There was another formally dressed guest in the room, a man standing by a television set at the rear of the room. He glanced at me and released his warm political grin. "Another outcast?" he said. "What's he got against you?"

"I'm rather surprised to see you in the White House at all, Senator Dempsey," I said as I strolled back toward the rear of the room.

He laughed his famous campaign laugh and said, "Gotta look the place over. Make sure he isn't packing the silverware." Despite the laugh and the apparent joking there was, as there always is in the good senator, that hard metallic under thread of, 'Don't get in my way, Buddy'."

"You do feel you have adequate support this time?" I asked.

"You're going to beat Old 76 at the convention?"

"You been reading the polls?" he said easily. "There's no such thing as a lead-pipe-cinch in politics, I learned that a long time ago, but right now it looks like I've got every state west of the Mississippi and north of the Mason-Dixon Line except Indiana. And don't be surprised if a few of the southern states that Old 76 thinks he's got in his hip pocket suddenly see the light and get with the winning side. Where you from?" He held out his hand, a motor reflex as automatic as his breathing.

"Portland, Oregon," I said smiling. "You hardly need to campaign in Oregon, Senator. We were with you four years ago and Old 76 hasn't done anything since to change our minds."

"Yep, the folks in the Midwest see that now too. If they'd been as smart as you folks in Oregon four years ago Old 76 never would've taken the nomination from me."

"It is too bad," I lamented with him. "His record on foreign affairs certainly has not been impressive. You're going to have your work cut out for you once you beat him for the nomination."

"You in politics out there in Oregon, Mr.-?"

"Waxout, Clifford Waxout. I—"

"Are you the Clifford Waxout of *America's Americans*?" he asked, reaching for my hand again. When I nodded, he said, "No wonder he dumped you from the reception line, Clifford. You folks at AA have really been giving Old 76 a rough time of it. You're dead right though, he is soft on Communism. He listens to those pin-stripe-suit idiots at the State Department and believes what they tell him about the Russians. I'm sure going to have to clean house over there at State when I get in. You can promise your people that, Clifford."

"Is this thing actually in color?" I said surprised. I was pointing at the TV set located just behind Senator Dempsey. On the lighted screen images were vaguely visible under shifting bands of green, blue, and red.

"Yeah, I was trying to adjust it," Senator Dempsey said as he started twisting one of the 15 or so knobs on the control panel. "I wonder where the hell Old 76 got this thing. There are not that many color TV's around. One of the things you gotta watch when you're in the White House is people giving you toys like this, expensive toys." The Senator's voice took on the cagey undertones of sly innuendo.

"Never know what a man wants from you when he suddenly turns too generous," he muttered as he concentrated on the control knobs. "But he's sure going to want something..."

"Hey," I said slightly startled, "this label plate on top of the cabinet says Crossfox Electronics. That's Martin Crossfox's company."

"Hmmm, I hadn't noticed that," the wily politician lied. "I'd heard Crossfox Electronics was working on color TV. Didn't know they had them on the market. Wonder what this number means: XM 4? Think that's the price?"

"In most companies XM means experimental model," I said, drawing on my years as a manufacturer of air conditioners. "I know Crossfox Electronics doesn't have a color TV on the market yet. This sure don't make sense." There you are, Senator, I believe you will find that Clifford Waxout is a suitably gullible audience for whatever political slight of hand you have in mind.

"Crossfox is pretty involved with *America's Americans*, isn't he?"

"He's Director of Southwest Division," I answered, still staring at the suggestive label plate. "I can't imagine how one of these would get here..."

"Yeah, it's funny," the good Senator remarked. "And funny Old 76 would keep it in this room too. I mean this room doesn't get used more than three-four times a year. All I know is Martin Crossfox hasn't sent me any color TV's."

Ah, Senator Dempsey, you are indeed an impatient man. You maneuvered us from speculation to indictment with startling abruptness.

"Oh, I doubt that Mr. Crossfox gave the set to the President," I protested in the kangaroo court. "The newsletter issued by Southwest Division is probably the most anti-administration newsletter of all the AA newsletters. They really get Old 76 about his pussyfooting with the Communists."

"Would you say Mr. Crossfox is politically ambitious? Hey, I've got a picture coming in. If I can just clear up this screen. Is he, Clifford?"

"Well sure. I mean I know Crossfox wants to be National Director of *America's Americans*. But, as you would say Senator, I think I've got the votes," I said grinning.

"Just between you and me, Clifford," he said nudging my arm with a playful elbow, "that's what I've heard; that you will be the next National Director. That's getting to be a pretty powerful slot here in D.C., National Director of *America's Americans*. You've got a lot of voters signing up with you because of your strong stand on Communism. And I like that."

"So I doubt that Martin Crossfox would be sending presents to Old 76," I summarized for the defense. "Martin is certainly ambitious, as you said, Senator, but he is also an honorable man. How else could he have become a millionaire?"

Careful, Augustus, the artist paints self-portraits with the brush, old man, not the mortar trowel.

"I guess you're right, Clifford. It sure would be what we in politics call *an unholy alliance*; Martin Crossfox and Old 76. Maybe Mr. Crossfox just wants Old 76 to come work for him after we 'throw the scoundrel out' as the old pols say. An ex-President of the United States on your Board of Directors sure doesn't hurt your corporation image-wise at all, at all. Yep, I think I've got those knobs figured now. Look at that picture coming in."

As Senator Dempsey—the man totally confident he was going to be the next President of the United States—as he adjusted the final tuning on the color TV he was still reserving an adequate portion of his brain for guarding his political life. He eased the last knife in rather gently.

"Too bad Martin Crossfox wasn't here tonight for Miss DiMartino's recital," he commented casually. "Be interesting to see if he got pulled out of the reception line by a Secret Service agent. Hey, there it is, the news broadcast."

Clifford, as you cavort with your salty friends in your Pacific Ocean playground, do you occasionally reflect on the harness of earthly burdens you have been permitted to slip? This latest, this apparent betrayal of *America's Americans* by your rival, Martin Crossfox, this too have you been spared. Ahh, Clifford, your debt to Augustus Mandrell, it continues to accumulate interest my son.

"Hey, that's Frank Kane of the FBI," Senator Dempsey said. "I know that son of a gun."

On the TV screen a youngish-looking, blond-haired man was being interviewed by three news commentators. The newsmen were seated side-by-side in the left lower corner of the screen, FBI man Kane sat alone at a desk in the upper right.

COMMENTATOR: "According to the press releases from your offices, Mr. Kane, all of the human parts of the young woman were removed to your FBI laboratories here in Washington?"

Good God, not more of this drivel Scott Balboa was so enamored with?

FRANK KANE: "Yes. Since the girl's head was discovered in the bus station locker in Louisville, Kentucky, one arm and leg in Bridgeport Connecticut, and one arm and leg in Lancaster, Pennsylvania, there was sufficient evidence to support the FBI's jurisdictional authority. The Bureau has a congressional mandate to step in whenever a judicious assessment indicates we are faced with an issue of malfeasance that is unintimidated by state boundaries."

COMMENTATOR: "Just when did the Bureau decide there was some connection between the dismembered parts of the young woman and this movie being made by the Hollywood producer, Harry Alucard?"

FRANK KANE: "The stenciling on the female leg found in Lancaster spelled out the words STEEL AROUND HIS NECK. Our

Los Angeles office advised headquarters that a movie of that title was being made in San Francisco by Mr. Alucard. We proceeded to question Mr. Alucard in San Francisco. The general content of his statement indicates his conviction that the duplication of wording is no more than an unexplainable coincidence. Thus far the Bureau has uncovered no evidence to indicate otherwise."

COMMENTATOR: "We have a piece of film coming up, Mr. Kane. It's part of a TV interview with movie producer, Harry Alucard, as he left your office in San Francisco following your questioning."

The three commentators Senator Dempsey and I were watching turned in their seats to look at a studio monitor. Mr. Frank Kane, the careful FBI representative, noted this shift in orientation and swiveled himself to look at the monitor. You're learning show biz fast, Frankie.

On the screen we saw bumping cameramen and trotting light holders bustle about the marble corridor of some governmental-looking building. The TV technicians and reporters were attempting to plug the path of a middle-aged man who was holding a straw fedora off to his side in an effort to block the bright lights from his eyes.

Harry Alucard came to a halt and determinedly faced the electronic hoard. Four hand-held microphones were thrust into the area six inches from Harry's mouth.

"I got nothing to say," Harry said, glaring around belligerently. "I just come from the FBI office and there I told them I don't know nothing about no dame in no lockers. There ain't even no scene in my movie about no dame in no locker. It's crazy. Wadda you people think I am, some butcher or something? I'm a movie producer. What am I suddenly—a Apache Indian with a tommyhawk cutting people's heads off? I use them lockers to put my suitcases in. Wadda I want to put a dame in there for?"

Mr. Alucard must be credited with total absorption in his dilemma. He had not once mentioned the title of his movie. They don't make the Hollywood moguls like they usta, lemme tell ya.

Several questions were machine-gunned at the harried producer by the reporters. One steel-edged voice finally slashed through the others:

REPORTER: "How could it be the same as your movie title, Mr. Alucard? This girl is being chopped up and stuck in lockers. How come the lettering on the girl's leg, how could it be identical to the title of your movie?"

ALUCARD: "How the (bleep) do I know?" (Recall, dear reader, that there was a wholesome time when one did not employ profanity in America's living rooms.) "Some pervert is running around cutting up some girl and renting lockers to stick her in. He could be writing anything on her leg. They can write the Lord's Prayer on the head of a pin, can't they?"

The reporters were less than dazzled by Harry's logic. The questions from the jostling newsmen poured in. The harsh-voiced chap with the knack for interview-shorthand again dominated:

REPORTER: "Coincidence? You calling it coincidence? A murderer is using the title of your movie, he's hacking a girl to pieces and using the title of your movie by coincidence?"

ALUCARD: "You know what I think? I think somebody's got it in for me."

Senator Dempsey started toward the TV screen again, apparently enjoying the role of color technician. "I'll tell ya who's got it in for you buddy, me!" He turned toward me, "When I'm in office, I'm cleaning house on barbarians like him." His piggy eyes gleamed. "I've made no bones about it, movie industry's got too much power. Freewheeling out of control. I've got a daughter, Mr. Waxout, a daughter..."

The news program cut away from the filmed interview of the persecuted Hollywood producer and switched to the three commentators and the FBI spokesman, Frank Kane.

COMMENTATOR: "According to news reports, Mr. Kane, that was the last time the FBI interviewed Mr. Alucard?"

FRANK KANE: "Yes. We are attempting to locate Mr. Alucard

for additional questioning. Thus far we have been unable to...ah, advise Mr. Alucard of our wishes."

COMMENTATOR: (the more belligerent member of the trio) "You can't find Alucard, isn't that the situation?"

FRANK KANE: "There is reason to believe that Mr. Alucard is taking refuge in his unalienable right to reinforce his privacy, yes."

COMMENTATOR (Let's-get-back-to-the-point-chap): "All of the evidence then was accumulated here in Washington and analyzed at the FBI laboratories. Has this centralizing of the investigation produced any conclusive results?"

FRANK KANE: "Yes. I'd like to use this chart to explain the situation."

The FBI man walked to a chart located to the right of his chair. Drawn on the chart was a round circle with a curved line surrounding part of the left side of the circle. A small dot was visible in the upper right quarter of the circle.

"What the heck?" Senator Dempsey muttered. "Oh, the head of a girl." He put his finger on the screen and traced his observation for me. "See, there's the head, the hair, and this dot is her eye. Profile view."

"Oh yeah," I said. "It's a girl's head. Usually TV doesn't make your brain work so hard."

"I can just see them now," Senator Dempsey chuckled, "over at FBI headquarters giving the illustrator his instructions. 'We want the head of a girl, but no gore. And for God's sake, no sex'. I suppose this outline of a key has to do with those keys they find with the parts of the body."

Several formally dressed men and women entered the recital room and moseyed over to join Senator Dempsey and myself around the television set. "My goodness, it's in color," one matron brightly observed.

On the screen FBI man, Frank Kane, used a short stick to tap at the drawing on the chart. "The woman's upper physical extremity, her head, was discovered in a bus station locker in Louisville,

Kentucky," he recapped. "A key was found clutched in the dental appointments of her head." He tapped the drawing of the key.

"This key, traced by the sequence of numbers appearing thereon, was used to open a locker in Bridgeport, Connecticut. This second locker was found to contain..." Mr. Kane paused as he removed the first chart, revealing a second chart underneath. On the second chart a human leg and arm was illustrated. The artist's talent had matured slightly. There was a curvature of the calf and thigh of the leg and the toes and instep were identifiable.

"...the intermediate and lower extremity limbs of a female," Mr. Kane continued, "the left arm and left leg were contained in the Bridgeport locker. Another key was found, tied to the big toe here. This key opened a locker in Lancaster, Pennsylvania where..." He unveiled the third chart.

"...another leg and arm were found. A series of words stenciled upon the appendages, words which, until this point in the investigation, contained minimal sequential continuity, and thus comprised subjective data for divergent interpretive conjecture, were..."

COMMENTATOR (interrupting): "You mean nobody knew what the words meant?" (The 'plain-speaking' member of the trio; sounding slightly impatient.)

"Yes," Mr. Kane said calmly. "We had been speculating on the meaning of the four words. The leg from the Lancaster locker contained the words in sentence form: STEEL AROUND HIS NECK. Now, we transported the evidence, the head, the two arms, the two legs, to Washington and had our experts brought in to apply their talents..."

"And their glue pots," a male voice in our group observed. A woman's voice immediately hissed, "Shush, Harold," to the amateur taxidermist.

Mr. Kane unveiled his fourth chart. The head, the two arms, and the two legs were illustrated thereon. The artist had refused to indulge his imagination, the central working parts of the maid were not even hinted at.

"It was at this juncture in the investigation that our experts uncovered a heretofore unsuspected complication," Mr. Kane continued, building a slight sense of melodrama. "When the evidence was thus assembled –" He tapped the chart showing the five parts, "...we discovered that the two legs did not properly support one basic predetermined assumption. You see, the two legs are both left legs."

COMMENTATOR: "You mean the legs do not match? No right-hand leg?"

FRANK KANE: "Gentlemen I am authorized to state that the Federal Bureau of Investigation is proceeding on the assumption that the Bureau is faced here with a possible homicide infraction of undetermined multiple occasion."

COMMENTATOR (old 'plain talking'): "You mean two women have been killed?"

"At least two," Mr. Kane conceded.

"Well, that certainly changes things," the matron standing next to Senator Dempsey said, with growing delight. "The story will be back on page one of the Post tomorrow."

Would you care to wager on that, my dear?

A polite, elderly Negro eased into our group and requested permission to turn off the TV set. "Mr. President is coming," the black man murmured. "Will you please take your seats."

As we broke up the TV audience, Senator Dempsey sought me out and said, "Let's get together after the recital, Cliff. I'd like to talk to you some more about the work you're doing with *America's Americans* and about how we can head off Martin Crossfox."

We ambled to our seats. All 76 guests appeared to be in place. Consuela DiMartino, I presumed was off in some holding area flexing her lovely diaphragm. There was a slight commotion at the door, the President swept in with the first lady on his arm. They were led up forward to the front row.

While the swarm noise was dying down I looked about at my seating companions. On my right was a rather plain, nervous-looking young man. Ah, but on my left was a vivacious young thing with a clutch of violets secured to her dress adjacent to one enchanting breast. Violets? Gadfry, it was the young lady from the world's record elevator ride! I glanced again at the young man on my right. No doubt about it, the same clumsy lad from the same vehicle.

"Why, hi there," the young lady said to the young chap, leaning out in order to direct her words past my chest. There was a degree of subterfuge involved in the salutation. Her words had spontaneity as though triggered by her sudden sighting of the young man. Actually her eye had been measuring him when I first looked at her.

She continued. "You didn't say you were coming here." To this quaint, but questionably chic, old place.

The recognition by the pert miss nearly unhinged the poor juvenile. He finally managed to blurt, "I didn't know you were headed here until I took the taxi behind yours and noticed that we followed your taxi all the way here."

Gad, was I to be subjected to this?

"Pardon me, my boy," I said to his claret face. "I believe I know your father. What is your name?"

"Ah...er..." He paused. The young miss and I stared at him unbelievingly as he bored smoking tunnels in his brain in an attempt to catch the elusive information, his name.

"Does it begin with an A?" I said helpfully. "B?"

"Bush," he blurted. "Woodrow Bush, Junior. Isn't that awful?" he said with an embarrassed laugh. "Your asking if it began with a B is what made it come out."

"How young you must be, Woodrow," I said chuckling kindly, "to be so terribly, terribly candid." I had leaned back in my chair so as to draw the young lady into our charming encounter.

"Do you know Dad?" Woodrow asked.

"Not unless he is among the deceased," I said. "The only Woodrow Bush I knew was a major in the Commandos in World War II.

Lost him when we went in after the giant squid factory in Dieppe. Damned good soldier...and now, my dear," I smiled at the girl, "you aren't going to disappoint an old man, are you? I have this eager young mustang here that is dying to be introduced."

The wide, rather pretty eyes held mine for a moment timidly. There was no indication that she recognized me as the impatient chap she had seen in the hotel elevator. Her memory appeared to be much more absorbed with young Mr. Bush, the florist with the flair for corsage arrangements.

The girl nearly looked for a decision from the rather prim aunt-type who sat on her other side, a woman of good bone who maintained an austere eyes-front but ears-cocked relationship with myself and the youths. But Marylou Lee chose to venture into the waters of adult decision making on her own, at least to the toe-dipping depth of delivering me her name, "I'm Marylou Lee," she said with touching bravery.

I introduced the two striplings formally. Then I insisted that Woodrow Bush change seats with me. He protested mildly.

"Actually I'm doing you an injustice," I said as we edged past each other. "Your chair is closer to the wall. The drapes there are designed to intensify the acoustics and when you have a performer with the range of Consuela DiMartino, acoustics is everything. I chance to be a...fan of the DiMartino." (Augustus, Augustus, do not permit those corrosive aromas of regret to seep about your resolve.)

From a practical point of view the relocation of Woodrow Bush from my right side to my left reflected sound containment tactics. First of all, I am not that partial to firearms. Guns come to you with an attached list of deficiencies: the oily steel, its stain and odor; the raucous, bragging announcement when discharged, the voice of the bully that testifies to one's presence, one's hiding place; your blind dependence on the precision contained in the gunsmith's hand, the munitions manufacturer's quality control practices; the concealment constraints, I mean Mother Nature has given us but two arm pits and they are within ready access to the rummaging of curious policemen; there is not even the need for him to bend over. Now the stiletto, on the other hand, a slender length of well-balanced steel, there is a delightful weapon; companion. Regarding concealment, the stiletto adapts to any number of irregularities in the human carcass, the sole of the foot, the recess between the shoulder blades, the inside of the thigh. But, you will recall from our earlier analysis of the successful presidential assassinations that the small handgun is unchallenged as the appropriate tool; an enviable track record.

Thus when I relocated the athletic-looking Woodrow Bush on my left, I had in mind rather more than escape from the long range mooning practices of he and Marylou Lee. While my left-handed dexterity in use of the pistol has not been found wanting, I am predominantly a right-handed person. My performance that evening of the near forgotten art of Shooting the President was to be a demonstration of the right-handed method only. Youths such as Woodrow Bush are frequently compensated for their mental awkwardness by possession of better-than-average physical coordination, an agility they can arouse with minimal forethought. Should young Woody choose to interrupt my labor, I now had my left arm free to deal with the busybody.

The seat next to Woodrow's (now next to mine) was occupied, incidentally, by a spidery old lady who was wired for supplemental hearing; hardly an adversary of formidable proportions. In fact I believe she slept through the complete performance, Consuela's and mine.

Marylou and Woodrow floundered conversationally as they searched for mutual college acquaintances. Since Marylou had attended the University of Virginia and Bryn Mawr and Woodrow had spent four years in the University of Colorado School of Mining, there was no hope. Marylou recalled that she had seen Colorado once on a trip to Los Angeles with her father, "The Colonel" but since they had been aboard a commercial airline at 18 thousand feet there appeared little chance that she had encountered any of Woodrow's classmates.

The young people persisted however and eventually found a subject of adequate inter-state scope. This was "The Case of the Girl in the Locker" as the Washington Post and the New York Times identified the story; "Locker Girl" for the readers of the headline-cramped tabloids.

Their discussion sifted the proposal that the affair was a publicity stunt for a motion picture. "I really don't know," Woodrow admitted, aligning himself thus with the best brains at the Federal Bureau of Investigation. "There are some peculiar guys out there in L.A. This producer, Harry Alucard, has a reputation for being pretty unsavory. You know what his name is spelled backwards, don't you?"

"I know Hollywood is a callous...well, institution," Marylou said with cute outrage, "but do you believe they would carry the proclivity to such extremes?" Ah youth.

Obviously Marylou and Woodrow devoted only surface interest to their conversation. The rubbing of their personalities across each other was the real game. As I eavesdropped on their so very earnest attempts to entrap each other I found myself wallowing in a nostalgic recall quite foreign to me. The magic of their mating ritual gradually mellowed me, even to the point of answering the tentative, bittersweet smile delivered to me by the lady on Marylou's left, a cordial signal of her own enchantment with the children. I even extracted myself from my calculations long enough to assess, through her tasteful voile gown, the flesh resistance and ligament anchorage of Marylou's companion. Although the encased parts had undergone 40-odd years of aging it was apparent that the Lee bloodline, assuming the lady was an aunt or near cousin, produced sound, resilient stock.

But—back to business.

At 8:10, a few minutes late, the First Lady arose and launched the evening's entertainment. The name Consuela DiMartino was eventually issued with a flitting, yet pedestrian, summation of the Diva's artistry. The room's lights were adjusted by an unseen hand to cast the audience in dimness while emphasizing the area adjacent to the grand piano with additional lighting.

Consuela's accompanist, a self-effacing vegetarian named Arlo, eased onto his seat in front of the keyboard. All eyes turned to the doorway at the side of the room. And the Prima Donna swept in upon us.

Her very carriage, the speed of her step, the cock of her elbow, the oscillation of the small fan strapped to her wrist, each was an item contributing to the mood appropriate to her first selection. Ah, the exhilaration of watching a true craftsman about his craft!

And, as the first note fled the Diva's lovely throat, my own precision timetable triggered irrevocably into being. I could permit Consuela but 12 ½ minutes of performance. She would gather the accolades generated by her first aria. She would unleash upon us her second. Then...rude interruption.

I touched the steel swaddled beneath my waistcoat. It was warm from the heat of my body. The minute hand of my watch moved with monolithic impersonality. The silver head of the president, six rows in front of me, silhouetted in the light about the piano, moved no more than an inch left or right.

Ahhh, but sir, your time has come.

My arm moved like a striking cobra to flip the simple, homemade device into the air. It soared, high and unnoticed, over the piano and into the portion of the room behind Consuela. The device struck the carpet. A strong white flash erupted accompanied by a sharp explosion like that of a tree trunk cracking open.

There was a stunned gawking and restlessness immediately around me. Consuela swallowed her last note as if struck. My dear....

Two husky gentlemen who had been prowling the sidewalls ran toward the still-glowing object on the carpet. Their frightened hands were under their jackets. Half of the audience was on its feet murmuring breathlessly. Old 76 was standing and had edged a bit behind his front row seat from which rostrum he was attempting to engage the gears of the Chief Executive decision-making process.

A narrow channel was open between he and I. He stood there at the end of this unpopulated fire lane, out in the open with naught to protect him but the tenuous supposition that when Man departed the jungle he left behind him his incivility.

"Hey, 76!" I cried to the Chief. He turned, his smile already spreading from the corners of his mouth.

I raised my pistol. "Et tu, Brutus?" I cried in hysterical outrage.

My finger was actually enjoining the trigger when a third party inserted himself into the contest. With uncharacteristic ill-timing, that adroit politician, Senator Rupert Dempsey, chose that precise moment to rise to his feet in the area between my pistol and the president, possibly to protest the impending damage to the rug of the house he planned to occupy.

Unhappily for the senator and his residential aspirations there was too great a coincidence between the upward lunge of his body and the trajectory of the one bullet I let fly. The bit of lead took the senator in a portion of the brain that proved to be somewhat fragile.

But my, didn't the cattle squeal and scatter. I ducked down and shouldered my way past the little lady on my right and those seated beyond her. I made my way to the draped sidewall encountering pleasant, shielding contact with several persons who, in the dimness were as anonymous to me as was I to them. I located the small door hidden beneath the draperies and slipped through. As I pulled the door softly into its frame, the lights were finally turned up to illuminate the chaos I'd left in my wake. (Or was it Senator Dempsey's wake?)

While my marksmanship was certain to be questioned, one could hardly find fault with my flight. I was precisely on schedule.

I scurried down one flight of narrow stairs, toured swiftly through two dark rooms smelling strongly of tradition, sidled past another door and ran along a corridor rarely seen by any but the domestics of the great house.

A burly man pushed himself out of the shadows up ahead of me at the end of the corridor and moved into a position to block my path.

I stopped a few feet from him and stared into his eyes with the same intensity with which he stared into mine. We stood thus for eight seconds. In that time only one of us spoke.

"You son of a bitch," he muttered, "You and me are going to have some talk one of these days."

He glanced at his watch, nodded, and unlocked the door at his rear. Even as I slipped out the portal he was swinging it shut to lock it on his side.

I moved now in the grass bordering a flagstone path outside the White House. I paused in a small square of shadow between the lawn flood-lamps that bathed the house in white light and reversed my dinner suit jacket. As I proceeded on into the lights I buttoned the garment to the neck. The inner lining was of dark blue with piping on the sleeves and additional military adornment, including two ribbons over the breast, to identify me as an officer of the British armed forces. A folded cap from the pocket reinforced my allegiance and rank. Commander D.P. O'Keefe of the 24th Bengal Lancers, at your service, sir.

As yet there was no visible indication that the perimeter security people had been informed of the four-minute-old tragedy within the White House. I strolled to the south exit and chanced (ha!) here upon a group of uniformed chaps who were in the progress of disbursing from that portal.

These were members of Her Majesty's Service who had been to a buffet supper and short briefing in the great house. During their briefing they had been treated to the pleasure of the President's company long enough to drink him a toast dedicated to British-American military harmony. The President had then left the Englishmen and hurried to the second floor for the DiMartino concert.

The British officers, when I encountered them, were making their way with a reserved level of joshing and high spirits toward the several limousines parked at the curb just outside the White House fence. What a happy sight they were to one of their own, stranded in this foreign capital far from the spit and polish of his crack regiment at home. If any noticed that their ranks swelled by one as they exited on to the sidewalk, returning the salutes of the American guards with appropriate casualness, if indeed any noticed, he did not speak. We English we are a reserved people, sir and, if your inquiry is directed into matters regarding the movement of our military personnel, you had damn well better present your security clearance papers and document your official need-to-know.

Despite his raging attack of homesickness D.P. O'Keefe, as disciplined a chap as you'd want to meet, did not join his fellow officers for the ride to their quarters at the Washington Navy Yard. Instead he squared his shoulders and walked off, a man dedicated to his lone mission. The great city swallowed him.

❧

One thing you must give the Americans credit for—they do know a good news story when they see it. See it? My God, this one, the attempted assassination of their president, was flung full upon their senses by every news media available!

In the first three days all matters of state, international and domestic, were suspended if not in fact at least in the minds of the citizenry. Even that most sacred of schedules, the baseball games, were suspended for three days. Of course an adjustment was hurriedly patched together, which permitted an extension of the normal season by a similar number of dates. For the average American in this period there was no world beyond his Atlantic and Pacific coastlines. He had a world of his own and tragedy stalked therein. He wished contact with no one other than his fellow citizens, his fellow mourners. And they were outraged, vengeful mourners indeed.

The name Clifford Waxout became overnight as well known as: Benedict Arnold, John Dillinger, bubonic plague. There was not a man in the land worth his salt, who did not swear, some publicly some in their shabby breasts, that should this animal Clifford Waxout come within the clutch of his bare hands there would be no recourse to Law, to sanity, to mercy. There would be only bloodletting, a bathtub full!

As much the opposite notoriety befell Rupert Dempsey. The senator had been rather well acclaimed during his lifetime. The nation's voters, as a matter of fact, according to the pollsters, were quite prepared to elect the man their next president. But his fame reached abnormal proportions following the "White House Incident", as the Russian press referred to the affair.

We do not often see a true martyr now a days. The occupation appears to have gone out of fashion or suffers for a lack of volunteers. In Rupert Dempsey the Americans then had a rare catch and, by George, they made merry with it.

Here was bravery of the highest order, demonstrated in the highest places, involving men of the highest positions. You don't get the slot machine to line up like that very often, Jack, let me tell you.

RUPERT DEMPSEY: HE GAVE HIS LIFE TO SAVE OUR PRESIDENT.

He was overnight, "The Fearless Senator Who Threw Himself Into The Path Of The Assassin's Bullet, Giving His Own Life To Save The Life Of His Major Political Opponent Because That Opponent Was, By The Voter's Wishes, The Chief Executive Of The United States." To quote one of the less prudent periodicals.

The newspaper and television industries, lacking a photographic record of the incident, and anticipating a demand by their subscribers for some nostalgic remembrance of the pageant, resorted to an ancient communications craft. Every chap with a bottle of India ink and an eye for perspective was pressed into the breach. The land was shortly inundated with "artists' concepts" of the kinetic affair. At first there were hurried pen-and-ink sketches, later a growing portfolio of oils and watercolors stained the marketplace.

Eventually that volatile denominator called "public taste" chose one painting as its favorite and to this day does it remain as the most accepted representation of the scene, appearing in every Anglo-Saxon encyclopedia and like periodical of any worth.

Personally, I have little quarrel with Martha Shriner, the artist of "Rupert Dempsey And The House He Never Lived In." I do not consider it an unforgivable affront that the shadowed figure of Clifford Waxout appearing in the lower right foreground of the painting, with the heavy jaw line and the really abnormally close-set eyes, radiates an aura of bestiality the candle-power of which I would be hard pressed to generate even under severe provocation. Had the circumstances been only slightly more prosaic, I would certainly have recommended litigation of some level or other on the part of Clifford Waxout's heirs.

No, my quarrel with the artist, if any, would center more on her departure from accuracy with regard to the figure of Senator Rupert Dempsey. My memory of the incident, and recall that I was positioned in an area from which it was possible to direct considerable attention to the tableau, does not include an observation of the senator's arms being outstretched, palms facing backwards toward the President. Nor do I recall the Senator's head as being cocked to one side with one masculine hirsute eyebrow arched high above an indomitable eye that glared at me with a lethalness equal almost to that of the flying bullet. Speaking of the bullet, Miss Shriner chose to record that moment in history during which the shot was passing from my pistol toward the President. The bit of lead is nicely sketched into the painting with a tantalizing obscurity that renders the fatal slug nearly visible, by far the artist's finest achievement.

Then of course there is too the figure of the President to consider when one becomes embroiled in the application of accuracy to the event. He is shown as standing behind Senator Dempsey. So far so good. But his posture, the forward tilt of the trunk, the hands rising from his sides, the mouth about to speak, the very slight touch of indignation (at being upstaged in this memorable moment by his political rival?) All of this, except possibly the indignation, is bogus. Those who read in the painting an interpretation that Old 76 was about to step forward and restrain Senator Dempsey ("No, no, old man, I believe the churl's argument is with me.") are deluding no one of significance.

On the morning following Senator Dempsey's demise the President decreed the period of national mourning. The famous, "I feel very humble" speech was seen on television by an estimated 50 million citizens, a record for that period. Even Old 76's most callous critics were struck mute by the response from the public. The American people and their Chief Executive became swaddled in a steel mesh of emotional rapport that only a very rash politician would choose to rattle.

And as the days passed with still no apprehension of the despicable manufacturer of air conditioners, the president, now enjoying the role of spiritual leader to the electorate, turned upon his law-enforcement agencies and demanded progress, success. "Aye!" cried the public.

The day of Senator Dempsey's funeral approached and still there was no indication that Clifford Waxout was about to be flushed. The indignation of the populace, impatient for their human sacrifice, blew frigid upon the man-hunters. "Find him! Find him! Find him!" chanted the mob.

The vilification was without foundation. The man-hunters, national and local, were engaged up to and flagrantly beyond, any peak of effort ever before generated. Which was as it should be, I suppose. In fact it was my anticipation of this unprecedented level of zeal on the part of the lawmen that had caused me to labor so to provide them a target for their enthusiasm. Pursuit of a flesh-and-blood lunatic like Waxout, as opposed to the chase of some nameless agent of gore, removed from the affair the dangerous ominous of professionalism; dangerous, that is, for the subscribers of Mandrell Limited and similar firms. We do not thirst for notoriety. Far better that the hounds should bay after the amateur assassin, Clifford Waxout, and all who might have been infected by his madness.

Mrs. Waxout, dear Nell, was naturally the first victim of legal harassment. She spent four days in a Portland, Oregon lock-up before the pleas of her physician gained her the comfort of "house arrest." Polly Culver was bustled off in an official vehicle as she deplaned in Portland after her homeward flight from Washington D.C. A brusk strike-in-the-night by a flying wedge of Federal vigilantes brought to many scattered jails nearly the entire hierarchy of *America's Americans*. Even Martin Crossfox, Director of Southwest, was visited at his massive Texas ranch by FBI agents using a rented airplane. But Mr. Crossfox's lawyers, who had been telephoned in New York, Los Angeles, and Houston ten minutes after the radio flash announcement of Clifford Waxout's name and deed, were in residence at the Crossfox ranch prior to the arrival of the FBI chaps. Sufficient areas for legal interpretation were identified in the papers tended by the FBI agents and they departed, without Martin Crossfox, to re-evaluate their Bureau directives.

The orgy of public blood-thirst rolled on for the better part of a week before it finally peaked and gradually spilled toward normalcy. Old 76 was, I believe, primarily responsible for capping the emotional gusher, although I am certain he had not intended to do so. The President was either treacherously advised, or was himself prone to wretched judgment. In his position I certainly would not have chosen the graveside ceremonies being accorded the late Senator Dempsey as the occasion to reveal to the nation the last, gasped words of the mortally wounded senator.

"I held him in my arms," Old 76 told us through our TV sets, "this brave senator. I could barely hear his words. The bullet was about its terrible labor. Then at last I made out the words. Senator Dempsey, using his final moment in this life, he said to me, "Chief, Chief, it's up to you now. You alone. You've got to carry that ball. Carry that ball, Chief..." Old 76 paused to blink back a tear. "Then he was gone," the Chief Executive continued hoarsely.

One almost heard the nation-wide click as many a shrewd old political head snapped to alertness, particularly those of the opposition party. It was obvious that the official mourning period in Washington D.C. had just been cancelled, abruptly and without warning. Politically speaking, it was back to business-as-usual.

And it was business-as-usual for Augustus Mandrell. The President's Poverty Commission contained a few more or less painful memories (Ah, Consuela...) Rather than steep myself in mournful recall I bustled out of Washington D.C. and flung myself about my business enterprise.

I'm certain, dear reader, that you can imagine the operational dilemmas faced by a firm such as Mandrell Limited. The nature of our service requires the use of some rather unorthodox marketing procedures. We have, for example, no home office. The city of London, and occasionally—when I cannot avoid it—New York City, are used as general bargaining arenas in which the initial haggling takes place. In lieu of a trained commercial staff we employ a group of customer-assistance personnel who work on a commission basis. In a typical evolution the customer initially seeks out one of these, well, "contact men" is the title that has gained the widest usage. If the contact man identifies possible grounds for fruitful negotiations (this relates much more to the customer's financial status than to the actual task) the customer is passed on to another contact man. Again, if the proposed commission does not violate any of Mandrell Limited's basic operational tenets, most of which relate to establishing the legitimacy of the customer's need, absolving him of any possible allegiance to a law enforcement agency, if these requirements appear to be in order, the customer is moved on to another contact man. Eventually when we have reduced the risk to an acceptable minimum Augustus Mandrell speaks to the applicant, frequently in an identity other than that of owner of the firm. Caution, my friend, is an art that requires practice.

Since The President's Poverty Commission had required my personal attention for a period well in excess of the norm, I found rather a surplus of 'buy orders' upon my arrival in New York City. Most were of a pedestrian nature: "Father has gone insane and is about to marry this common fan-dance person, Rose E. Velt. We can't have the family name—and fortune—being dragged down by some strip-tease wanton." Myself: "You would rather that Miss Velt were no longer...available?" "Well...ah...that's one answer of course. But that's no guarantee that father will not do something equally stupid before he dies." Myself: "I see."

(Incidentally, I'm certain those of you that are familiar with the enviable record established by the Belfast Repertory Players in France during World War II are now heartened to learn that at least one member of the cast, Miss Rose E. Velt, is doing so well. Those of you that are not familiar with the Belfast Repertory Players and the foxhole fandangos demonstrated by the ladies of the group need not despair. A rather lucid account of the Players and their hedgerow hi-jinks is available in a journal of mine titled: THE GENERAL LA CORTE COMMISSION.)

As I said there were numerous enterprises awaiting my attention in New York and they reflected, in content, a rather gray repetition of past commissions: "My wife refuses to give me a divorce and I'm absolutely insane about this garbage man."

There was one petition, however, that was spring-loaded with promise and haunting memory. A man named Pierre Brichant had talked to two of my contact men. One of the two, Valentine Somosa, a hairdresser in a Fifth Avenue beauty salon, told me about Monsieur Brichant prior to our agreement.

"This customer, Brichant, is a teaser," Valentine said over the telephone. "He's one of those exciting French existentialist types. You know, pudgy and bald with these great inner caverns full of introspective pornographic wellsprings? Utterly delicious man."

Valentine, conversationally, was somewhat of a trial but he

brought several invaluable assets to his assignment with the firm. He was an acute diagnostician of personality. Valentine could smell a cop through a Harvard accent or beneath the drool of a mumbling spastic. The hairdresser possessed also a hairline tolerance for this issue we call ethical behavior; tolerance, yes; adherence, no.

"Anyway, Brichant is in opera," Valentine continued. "As just who isn't now-a-days? He's manager to that Prima Donna, Consuela DiMartino. Poor thing. You've heard what happened to Consuela? How the Washington fuzzy wuzzies have her in their cattle pens? Did you read about it? You know, sir, I'm always appalled by your fantastic disinterest in current events. Remember that commission two years ago? You didn't even know who the Isabel Brady Dancers were. You really should have somebody read you the full New York Times every morning. I—"

"Has Monsieur Brichant called about the commission?" I interrupted. "Have you heard from him since his problems in Washington?"

"Oh Great Caesar," Valentine moaned. "How eternally incisive. Now, now, don't hang up on me. I have a few rare tidbits to go. First, no, Brichant has not called. I imagine he's positively perspiring all over Washington trying to protect the DiMartino from the goon squads. The Secret Service and the FBI are evidently convinced Consuela brought that idiot with the defective eyesight to the recital on purpose. Did you ever hear of anything so bungled? One of my friends last night remarked that if Clifford Waxout had gone into the Ford Theater he'd have shot Mrs. Lincoln. Isn't that wild? I told him it wouldn't have been a bad idea."

He paused, waiting for me to speak. The silence was alive with tension. Silence always would be for Valentine. He incidentally had not been involved in the negotiations that brought The President's Poverty Commission to the firm.

"All right, just for that," he sulked, "I'll conclude this conversation with a plea for more money so utterly groveling it will melt whatever organ it is you use for a heart. And yes, yes, I'll call and leave you a message as soon as I hear from Monsieur Pierre Brichant. Which I'm positive will occur just as soon as he has a free moment. For one thing he was quite taken with me. For another, he seems absolutely desperate to find Harry Alucard before the police do."

"You had that financial business looked into?" I asked. "We know for certain that Consuela DiMartino's corporation—Conmar Enterprises—has money invested in Harry Alucard's movie company?"

"Oodles and oodles of money," Valentine giggled. "Isn't that wild? The world's greatest opera singer investing in Harry Alucard's horror movies. Did you know Harry's movies are all the rage in my neighborhood right now? No one will listen to you at a party unless you can quote the frightened postmaster in THE RABID MAILMAN or the Southern sheriff in HARVEST OF BLOOD. Everybody is just dying to see STEEL AROUND HIS NECK."

"You and your friends may have to wait for some time," I commented. "If the police find Mr. Alucard it is doubtful that he will have the leisure for film making. Isn't that Pierre Brichant's estimate?"

"Of course. But I don't see how the police can possibly tie Harry Alucard to that grotesque business of the girl-in-the-locker. My God, the man would have to be insane to go out and hack up—what is it now? At least two ladies just to promote his film. I mean, fun's fun and all that in little old Hollywood, but—butchering?"

"Obviously somebody is insane," I said. "All right, if Pierre Brichant contacts you pass him on to Dr. Cooper immediately."

"But of course, Master," he said, surprised. "You know something I don't know, is that it? Why should Monsieur Brichant see Dr. Cooper first? All right, all right, preserve your everlasting reticence. This absurd business! But just tell me this one thing: is our stolid Dr. Cooper a Negro? That deep primordial voice with that slur just dripping with iron fillings. Whenever I talk to him my very cuticles itch. Is he black?"

"Didn't a woman named Butler come to see you?" I asked.

"God, you are implacable. Yes, she did. But you've been missing so long recently; at least I haven't been able to raise you, that Mrs. Butler took her business elsewhere. How a woman in her social position survives with a name like that devastates me."

"When you say, 'Mrs. Butler took her account elsewhere', where do you mean?" I asked, deliberately withholding my real concern from my voice. "Do you mean to Tokyo? To Mr. Roman Wakamotsu?"

"No, no, I have the eerie impression the man she went to is here in New York. Wouldn't that be wild? Two of you? And it wasn't only Mrs. Butler. Remember Count Malesich and his heiress wife? He also bolted the flock. Said his timetable was inflexible, had to be rid of her before the season opened at Majolica. He commissioned someone else and I have the very tingly impression the Count went to the same person Mrs. Butler went to. Me suspects, Master, there is a competitor in the area."

"Do you know anything about him?"

"A few cute whispers only thus far. That New York is the place to reach him. From the evidence I'd say he is not some crude gangster type. Mrs. Butler's twin sister, the one with the eye for chauffeurs and bus boys, expired two weeks ago, presumably from injuries suffered when thrown from her horse. Count Malesich's heiress was attended to also. She is thought to have fallen off their yacht somewhere south of the Bahamas. Both very neat. Whoever our competitor is, he is certainly not garish."

The next evening the subject of Mandrell Limited's competitor was again under dissection.

"Frankly, I find it unsettling," Dr. Cooper said. "I doubt that the market will support two firms. That is, the market catered to by Mandrell Limited."

"You have heard no rumors then?" I asked. "Other than vague references to another firm? Is there any possibility the Mafioso has decided to expand their execution practice into—let us call it, 'the quality market'?"

"Lordy no," Dr. Cooper said. "They are smart enough to recognize that they have their side of the street, you have yours. When the assignment becomes any more complex than the folding of an insolvent bookmaker into the trunk of an abandoned car they have no expertise."

We, the doctor and I, were seated in a small apartment located over his drug store on the west side of Manhattan close to the Negro ghetto, Harlem.

"Can you imagine any Neapolitan 'torpedo' being assigned that White House business?" Dr, Cooper continued chuckling. "Or I believe the street term is now 'hit man'. Those crazy Wops would have tried to do it from a speeding black Cadillac with blazing machine guns."

"You must admit, Doctor, they are rather effective. I believe I have read that in any given year citizens of the city of Chicago expire from the classic 'over-dose of lead' at a rate exceeding one-a-day."

"But no class, Man, no class," the Doctor objected. "They underbid each other. 'If Tony will do-a da job for 300 bucks, I'll tell-a you wot. I'll do it for 250, if you buy da bullets.' How you going to get class when you're shopping around for the lowest bidder?"

"My dear, Doctor, are you questioning the 'free enterprise' system? The very cornerstone of America's greatness?"

Dr. Cooper laughed and shuffled in his worn slippers to the refrigerator to get us two more cans of beer. "That's one side of Capitalism, Mr. Mandrell," he preached. "There's another side. There is always the situation where the customer has a requirement involving spell-binding complexity. Now that's where we come to the 'sole source' side of Capitalism. There's only one firm that can handle the order, no competitive bidding. The capitalistic feature remaining at this point is the negotiating, the haggling. You—Mandrell Limited—estimate the risk, you set your price. The customer—like our friend Mr. Coffee—can accept, reject, or haggle. I suspect that Mr. Coffee was a good haggler?"

"He was indeed, Doctor. But then Mandrell Limited is not without experience in that sort of thing. I believe you will be quite pleased with the amount of your commission. Especially with the addition of this titillating bit of cash," I patted the rather chubby envelope inside my jacket pocket that Dr. Cooper had handed me upon my arrival, "from Monsieur Pierre Brichant. Senator Dempsey would have made messy business for CONMAR ENTERPRIZES it seems. Quite a bit of legal altercation for the esteemed Mr.Harry Alucard." And, true to the domino effect dear Consuela, would evaporate your petulantly lavish life style. Good god Mandrell, is there no end to your compassion for the lass?

"Ah, that explains Mr. Brichant's rush. It sounded as if he was hard pressed to get to Hollywood. As to my restitutions, I'm sure your allocation will be sufficient. You may have your faults, Mr. Mandrell—I am told we are none of us without blame in the eyes of the Lord—but one thing you do not do is you do not degrade your talent by expending it for less than its true worth."

As you may have guessed, dear reader, I kinda liked old Dr. Cooper.

"You haven't seen Mr. Coffee yet, have you?" Dr. Cooper asked seriously. "I mean, I've got the impression –old southern instinct—that you've been out of town. That you didn't come straight to New York from Washington."

I stared at him over my can of beer and said nothing.

"I ain't asking you your business, Mr. Mandrell," he protested lightly. "It's just I got me some bad feelings. Things don't feel right since that night in the White House. And Mr. Coffee was sure upset that I couldn't put him in touch with you last week."

"I was down in Texas, Doctor," I said quietly. "My stay was rather longer than I had anticipated."

In truth I was collecting my dues from the rather unyielding Mr. Martin Crossfox, head of the America's Americans Southwest Division. Apparently he had second thoughts about the monetary value of becoming a shoe-in for the National Directorship of the institution and the agreed upon particulars of having Mr. Clifford Waxout tidily out of the picture. A disenchantment I suspect brought on by, as I believe he so succinctly put it, "The greatest institutions dedicated to national security ever created closing in on me like pigs on shit."

Untidy, but profoundly accurate.

I had a dishearteningly bothersome time convincing the chap that this indeed was not my problem. Payment was thusly extracted under a mortifying display of unnecessary duress; payment for the demise of Mr. Clifford Waxout. Almost of its own will, my hand trembled and my fingers crushed my beer can. We understand, don't we, dear reader? We who are haunted by the numbing details of the Back From The Dead Commission.

"Tomorrow," I said. "Tomorrow I will see Mr. Gundar Coffee. Your portion of the fee should be in your hand by next week."

"I'm not worried about my fee, Mandrell," Dr. Cooper said roughly. "I mean I'm not worried about the one I got coming. I'm worried about the fees I'm counting on. The ones in the future. I let myself absorb a lot of obligations since I come in with you—"

"Such as the two young ladies in that apartment in the Apollo Towers?" I remarked, unfriendly.

"Damn right," he snapped. "And a little hustle I got going along the street here that needs development, needs cash. So I don't want to see Mandrell Limited out of operation. And Mr. Gundar Coffee is the kind of man that can pull the gears and the springs out of any machine and burn the paint off with a blowtorch. I tell you, he's easy to talk to. Got this nice earthy vocabulary that gives you the impression of breezy sincerity. But, Mr. Coffee, he don't deal in sincerity. I'll bet he doubts its existence. I've met some bad asses in my time, but I'll tell you, this Gundar Coffee is as ruthless as an avalanche."

"Doctor, Doctor, of course he is," I protested reasonably. "Had he not been I would never have accepted his commission." I stood up.

"You be careful with him, Mr. Mandrell," Dr. Cooper said as we walked to the door of his apartment.

"And you be careful with your exercise at the Apollo Towers, Doctor," I smiled. "Two of them in the same apartment. Interesting."

"Well, you all know how it is," he said dragging up a Bayou accent. "Them sweet little ol' things, day is twin sisters; Xeno an' Zennona. Ah couldn't bring myself to break up the matched set."

The small airliner eased below the nasty looking gray line of clouds and flew toward the runway through the heavy drops of rain. It was the commuter flight from New York's LaGuardia airport with 12 passengers on board. The landing was smooth despite the water that splashed up over the landing gear as the pilot reined the craft to the reasonable speed of the concrete runway. The blurred, silver, propellers chopped the Newark, New Jersey airport raindrops as the plane taxied to the terminal.

Twelve passengers deplaned. Eight of them rushed across water puddles to the shelter of the terminal. Four men walked at a slower pace from the craft, their minds on some thought more distressing than the dampness in their faces.

As the four approached the waiting room door, I stepped out with an airline umbrella open over my head. "Mr. Coffee?" I inquired of the gaggle.

Gundar Coffee looked at my blue jacket with the airline insignia stitched over the pocket. "I'm Mr. Coffee," he said businesslike.

"The captain of the plane you just came in on, Mr. Coffee, he has a message for you," I said, excited. "He got it on his radio and called control. Said it's important." I moved past Coffee toward the aircraft then turned and tilted my umbrella inviting him to join me under its protection.

He hesitated then looked at the other three men and snapped,

"Two of you wait inside. Harry, you stand by out here." He walked with me to the airplane but waved off my offer of the umbrella. Takes more than a little God damn rain to bother Gundar Coffee, Jack.

Coffee climbed the three steps to the cabin ahead of me. I folded and shook out the umbrella before following him into the empty cabin.

"Well, get your pilot out here," Coffee said nodding at the door to the cockpit. The aircraft seated twenty passengers. The interior of the cabin was constrictive; one kept one's head bent to avoid contact with the overhead.

"Ah, Mr. Coffee, please sit down," I said, discarding my tense, airline-clerk voice. "We will be taking off in thirty seconds."

A mechanic in raingear jumped from his baggage-pulling tractor outside and closed the door to the craft. The click of the double-acting lock was quite loud.

The door to the cockpit opened and the co-pilot stuck his head out. "Everything okay, Mr. O'Keefe?" I nodded. "Okay, fasten your seatbelts. We'll be moving out to the runway." He closed his door, which also sounded a metallic locking device.

"Mandrell?" Gundar Coffee said looking closely at me, searching through my youthful face for a face he'd seen before. He had opened the middle button of his raincoat and the end of his right sleeve abutted the gap in the raincoat's button line. The hand from said sleeve was about some business of its own inside the raincoat.

"Of course, Mr. Coffee," I assured him. "I would hardly entrust the final payment of my fee to a junior member of the firm. Ah, I suspect that when your friends in the waiting room see the aircraft is about to depart they may initiate some rash action. I recommend that you signal them to apply their dedication elsewhere. Are they Secret Service?"

"Christ, no," he said as he bent to look out a window. "The last guys I want meeting you are Service guys."

The man Mr. Coffee had left to stand in the rain outside the waiting room was running toward the mechanic driving the tractor, yelling and waving at our aircraft.

"Call them off, Mr. Coffee," I said harshly. "This business is between you and me."

Coffee stared at me with his frigid bureaucratic eyes. The two engines outside revved up, biting the cold New Jersey air to pull the aircraft away from its parking space. We started to move.

Mr. Coffee spit over the backrest of the seat in front of the one in which he sat. He leaned his face to the window and waved to his men with a short, palm-down waving motion. Several interpretations could be applied to Coffee's hand gesture, but basically it was one that said, "Take it easy. Lay back. Our turn will come."

We did not speak again until the engine vibration mellowed as we took our place in line for take-off.

"Pretty damn cute, Mandrell," Coffee said. "What the hell's wrong, don't you trust me?"

"It must be obvious that I trust you, Mr. Coffee. My escape from the White House last week was somewhat totally in your hands. Happily you were at that service door as scheduled to permit me to exit the White House lawn."

"What do you mean, 'somewhat totally' in my hands? What would you have done if I wasn't there? Or if I'd been there with a few Secret Service boys?"

"Those were your options, of course. But I dare say I'd have found some way to open the portal had you been absent. As for the presence of you and the Palace Guardsmen, wouldn't you have been hard pressed to explain your prior knowledge of the escape route?"

"Don't worry, I could've explained it. And it sure would have saved us all this grief we got now trying to find Clifford Waxout. Nailing you there in the White House would've made life a lot easier."

"By 'nailing' I presume you mean with massive fire-power. 'Riddled with bullets', isn't that the preferred American solution to complex issues of personality conflicts?"

"It sure avoids a lot of bullshit, Pal."

"Mr. Coffee, you informed me during our initial meeting several months ago that you learned of the existence of Mandrell Limited from some Federal Bureau of Investigation file to which you evidently have access."

"FBI has a file on you that would trip an elephant."

"Yes, well I suppose the Bureau must always have some objective in mind. I mean all those tax dollars spent and man hours invested—"

The aircraft engines roared again to a purposeful volume of clatter, quite overpowering our ability to communicate. We were taking off. The farmlands of New Jersey were painted over by gray, mean-looking clouds. At 8,000 ft. we broke into the clean, blue sky above the clouds. The pilot leveled off and the internal combustion brutes in the wings were brought to heel by a skillful withdrawal of their petroleum feed.

" Where are we headed?" Mr. Coffee asked. "Back to La Guardia Airport in New York?"

"I thought we'd fly down the coast a bit," I said. "Lovely countryside."

"You think I might have some more guys posted in La Guardia?" he asked grinning.

"It's possible. After all, you thought I would be boarding this aircraft this morning at La Guardia airport when you did."

He chuckled and said, "You should have seen me eyeballing all the passengers on the flight over to Newark trying to figure out which one was you. So you chartered the plane for this afternoon. You're a careful guy, Mandrell."

"Yes, Mr. Coffee, very. That is the intelligence you should have absorbed from reading those FBI files."

"That's why we hired you, Pal."

"That is also why you should not trifle with me, *Pal*. That escort of ruffians you brought with you, their number hardly reflects what might be termed, 'bargaining in good faith'. Mandrell Limited has been in the business for a number of years. We would hardly have survived if we did not recognize the hazards associated with collecting our fee."

"Sure," Mr. Coffee laughed, "human nature. Once you knock the guy off, Christ the customer don't need you. You're the guy with his hand out, presenting the bill. And—the real messy part—you know the inside story. Blackmail and the like. Witness for the Prosecution if the thing ever got in front of a jury".

"I have no way of knowing what editorial comments, what conjecture your FBI may have appended in their files," I said. "If they indicate that Mandrell Limited resorts to blackmail, the files are in error. Aside from the ethical factors involved it would just be too much of a bloody nuisance. Monthly payments, accounts receivable, accounts overdue, solicitor action, receipts, those odious little chit books- to be enclosed with your 'remittance'. No, no, sir, the 'lump payment' is by far the preferred approach. Speaking of which....?"

"Yeah, well, we'll get to that," Mr. Coffee said, leaning back comfortably in his seat. "First, let's talk about the nuts and bolts of this thing at the White House. I really gotta hand it to you, Mandrell. You do know your stuff. I never saw a more natural fall guy than this jerk, Clifford Waxout. Where the hell, did you ever find him? With that crackpot outfit *America's Americans* hanging around his neck we can nail him with everything from the assassination, to the Washington debt, to the Washington Senators being sixth place."

"Your Senators in Washington? They're in sixth place to whom?"

He was startled for a moment. Then he chuckled and said, "Not our senator Senators. Our baseball team Senators. Yeah, I don't know where you found Clifford Waxout but he's perfect. But, Buddy, you gave me one hell of a fright that night. Why the hell didn't you call me and tell me you were set? I wasn't even sure you were in the audience."

"There appeared little reason to involve you, Mr. Coffee. I did not require your assistance, other than as guardian of the exit door. And to ensure the British Military personnel departed from their briefing on schedule."

"No, that's not the way I operate, Mandrell. I don't like guesswork and I don't put up with it from any of my people."

"Happily for your managerial convictions you need no longer include me as one of 'your people'. Now, if we can get to the purpose of this—"

"So, you think it's all over between you and me do you? Christ, I'm sounding like some lovesick song. Maybe like a song your cutie-pie opera singer would sing. Man, you had me sweating that night. I went over and over that damn guest list looking for you. There were about ten people on the list we didn't know much about, including Clifford Waxout. Then it got real sticky. We had a burst of last-minute cancellations. Like the Chief Justice, Don Wood, and his old lady down with the flu. That meant throwing in new names. The total always has to come out 76. When I saw the new list I thought I had you spotted. There was a guy named Woodrow Bush in there who looked shaky. You know, no real clout in Washington, just a nephew of some old pol from the boondocks. But you fooled me, Mandrell...Not many people fool me, Pal."

"I can well believe that, Mr. Coffee. Evidently you were advised about Clifford Waxout's political leaning? He was not permitted to shake the hand of the host."

"Oh sure. Secret Service dug up that *America's Americans* background the day after Miss DiMartino submitted Waxout's name as her escort. Secret Service even recommended Waxout be dropped from the list. I had to veto the blackball purely on the chance Waxout was Augustus Mandrell. I told them it would be an unwarranted insult to the Prima Donna. Don't think I haven't taken a bushel of flack for that. How the hell did you ever fake the DiMartino into bringing you to the party?"

"Have you made any effort to get Miss DiMartino released? You must realize that she was not involved."

"Not me, Jack. Not on your life. That's walking around with your fly open. Get it straight in your head, Pal; there are a lot of guys in D.C. who got more than a doorknob under their hat. We got a lot of guys that are always looking for the piece of the machine that makes the piece they can see go round. And don't kid yourself, Senor Mandrell, we are not away clean on this thing yet. Not by a damn sight."

"That is rather obvious," I sighed.

"Wadda you mean?"

"I mean that you are without the one item that would cause me to assume our contract has reached a satisfactory termination. You have no briefcase, no attaché case. Even considering the compact dimensions of your American banknotes it does not appear feasible that you could carry the sum involved on your person. I would guess that that bulge under your raincoat is not a money belt but rather an omen of the mutual trust you enjoy with your fellow man."

"My, my. We sound a little bitter. And after you went to all this trouble with the airplane double shuttle." His chuckle was not exactly humanitarian in tone, nor was it meant to be.

As you may have guessed, I did not particularly like Mr. Gundar Coffee. There was about the gentleman the aura of gray dungeon walls, the sense of rusty iron rings imbedded between large damp stones.

"That's right, Mandrell, no payoff. I got about 105 bucks on me. Enough for a good steak dinner tonight, a bottle of Jack Daniels in the hotel room, and maybe one of them high-class New York pieces of ass."

"Mr. Coffee," I said, exerting a remarkable level of restraint, "during one period of my life I entered into a contract with the British Government. Something to do with a German general, which is neither here nor there. Now, for some reason the British Government—my own government—chose to default on their financial obligation. Mr. Coffee, before the whole affair was concluded—and concluded unsatisfactorily, I might mention, for I was never reimbursed—not only was the German general among the deceased but so too was a Royal Air Force sergeant and a Special Services Army sergeant. Additionally, The RAF suffered the loss of an operational bomber and two flight officers were in a German prisoner of war camp. I submit, sir, that all of these losses—with the exception of the German general—were unnecessary. They were due to a lack of trust, a lack of integrity, a lack of mature judgment, regarding the irrevocable nature of a business obligation with the firm of Mandrell Limited."

(Please, dear readers, do you understand now? Will you henceforth cease your demands on me for a published account of The German Invasion Expert Commission. It must be obvious from the skeletal detail presented above that the rancor, the bitterness has yet to be laid to rest. Age, so I am told, mellows even the most harsh memories. If so, perhaps, someday...)

"Who said anything about not paying you?" Mr. Coffee exclaimed, both hands out, palms up, in a gesture of mild rebuttal. "It's just that the job ain't finished yet. Christ, we're good for the money. I mean just because you got heisted by your own government... Incidentally, that is a pretty story, the bomber, the pilots, the sergeants, real pretty. Remind me to have you in for a drink sometime and I'll tell you about me and the Japs in the Pacific. We can match medals."

"Please explain your terminology," I snapped. "'The job ain't finished yet'. Precisely what do you mean?"

"'It's a long, long time from May to September'," Mr. Coffee said, crooning the lyrics from some simplistic ballad. A small edge of my attention observed, with a start, that the man had a rather good singing voice. "And it's a long time from making a deal and getting your hands on the money. We got us a little problem, Mandrell."

"I will insist that you justify that pronoun 'we', Mr. Coffee."

"Yep, *we* got us a problem. Christ, I've never seen anything like it. The hunt for your boy Clifford Waxout has turned into a Roman Circus. They've dug up everybody he ever spoke to. There's wire taps on every other house in Portland, Oregon. There's agents, cops, private eyes, deputies, marshals, Junior G-men, anybody with two eyes, staked out watching every place he ever lived in, ever visited, ever talked about. Doctor's offices, churches, every company he ever sold an air conditioner to, even his God damn grammar school in a place called Willowick, Ohio, they're all covered. And now it's worse, spreading out overseas. It turns out Waxout took a trip to Europe and you know where he went? Moscow! Now we got a Commie agent on our hands. Is that true? Was he a Commie underground agent? Is that why you picked him?"

"How certain are you of your information?" I asked carefully. "In the initial phases of any investigation there is bound to be a degree of rash conjecture."

"Nope. We got the passport, the visa. We've got every piece of official paper ever issued on Waxout, Clifford F. Secret Service has the collection in a special room over at the Treasury. They've pulled in everything: All his corporate records from the air conditioning factory. All his personal correspondence from his home, his *America's Americans* files, his medical records, his college transcripts, even some old love letters we found from some French chick named Jeannie Champlain he met overseas during the war. Evidently old Clifford did quite a bit of playing around. We've got testimony from a young girl who worked for *Americas Americans* in Portland that Clifford and the Secretary of Northwest, a Polly Culver, had something going. Did it right in the office during working hours. You get in on any of that?"

"I fail to see how the diligence of the law enforcing agencies affects our contract."

"The body, man. The body. We gotta have Waxout's body. Christ, you didn't burn it did you?"

"There was no mention of this requirement in our original negotiations."

"Hell I know that. I forgot how bloodthirsty the American public could get. And the longer they go without their pound of flesh the more they're going to say, 'What could have happened to Clifford Waxout? A man just can't disappear. Not with his picture in every paper in America and no friends.' Then, Pal, the little bell will ring. Then they figure there's one way a guy could disappear. Dead-and-buried disappeared. But dead and buried means somebody to do the burying. Then it's not Waxout they're looking for it's the guy with a shovel. It's no longer a one-man operation. It's a Goddamn conspiracy and that's when you and I are in deep shit."

"Mr. Coffee, stay out of Washington for a few days," I advised casually. "Your over exposure to the panic within the law enforcement agencies has distorted your view."

He shook his head. "They have a right to panic. I thought this thing would die down when we buried Senator Dempsey last Friday. It ain't. The public wants its murderer, and wants him bad."

"I disagree. While the Americans are indeed a vindictive people they are also an easily distracted lot. The fluctuations in the baseball world or the peccadilloes of some Hollywood personality will shortly absorb their thirst for blood."

"Balls! The only thing that'll cool them off is Clifford Waxout hanging by the neck from the top of the Washington Monument. You're the one that's out of touch, Mandrell. You think you can sit on your ass here in New York counting your money? Well, Buddy, you should see some nice little letters that have landed in the Secret Service mailroom. Real cute they are. So cute they've got me pissing in my pants." He paused and glared at me. He appeared to be waiting for a reply, to what I have no idea.

"Perhaps you are easily impressed," I commented.

"You'll be Goddamn easily impressed," he yelled. "I've seen two of the letters. They both say the same thing. They say: 'If you want to find the man who murdered Senator Dempsey, look for the man who put the girl in the lockers. It's the same man.' How's that for cute?"

"I fail to track with you, sir," I said shaking my head. "I assure you, that girl, or girls, in-the-locker business is not a Mandrell Limited commission. Bloody tasteless mayhem."

"Mandrell, do you know what a 'mandrill' is?"

"Unhappily, yes. A rather large African baboon. Reportedly ill-tempered."

"Yeah and you know how these letters I'm talking about are signed? With the drawing of a monkey face and a signature saying: THE MANDRILL!"

A long slender tube with attached fishhooks slid up the inside of my spine.

"You change one letter in that signature and you blow this thing wide open," Gundar Coffee continued to spout his acid-bubbling tidings. "Thank God there's so much mail coming into Secret Service they can't keep up with it; people claiming they saw Waxout in every state of the union. And thank God Secret Service is frightened that the silly FBI will take over the whole show. There's some Bureau boys who would know what the 'Mandrill' means if they saw those letters. They know Augustus Mandrell over at FBI. You even got some fans over there, couple of agents who think you're a regular Mandrake the Magician. But they'd nail your ass in a minute if they ever got the chance."

"Where did the 'Mandrill' letters come from?"

"One postmarked New York City, the other Washington D.C. And that's no Goddamn coincidence, using the name Mandrill. He knows you, Buddy. He knows you did the job at the White House, not Clifford Waxout. There's been a leak. I figure it's at your end, one of those contact men in New York I talked to before I talked to you."

"Don't be an ass!"

"Yeah? Well, it wasn't at my end. Only two people in D.C. know the score and you can bet your seersucker neither of us is talking."

"And I am the only person at my end that knows the details,

Mr. Coffee. You were sufficiently intelligent to refuse to provide my men anymore than a hint at the exact service you wished. Your near total reticence, incidentally, brought your petition to my attention rather sooner than—"

"Yeah, yeah, never mind the bouquets. Maybe I didn't spill my guts to your boys but I think that doctor, the black guy, I think he recognized me. I mean, Time magazine has had my picture a couple of times, and Newsweek. Your black doctor struck me as a pretty sharp cookie who'd keep up with the news."

"Dr. Cooper would hardly be of use to me if he were an imbecile."

"I wouldn't trust him across the street. These upstarts get a few books under their skin, a little Tom Pine and Dos Passos –" Mr. Coffee's eyes glittered as he slid his dormant erudition into me like a knife. "and they start looking at a quick mugging in Central Park as an exercise in social justice. Any white man they can kick in the balls is a step forward for 'equal rights'. For my money your black associate is our letter writer. And if you don't want to take care of him, I'll take care of him."

"You will keep your fat hand out of the affairs of Mandrell Limited, Mr. Coffee, or I assure you it will be peeled to the bone. Dr. Cooper could hardly have recognized you when you met. Dr. Cooper is blind, totally blind. The affliction was delivered to him by the lead weight encased in a police department truncheon. Dr. Cooper is one of the last people who would provide any assistance to any law enforcement agency. Therefore look to your own organization for the Judas."

Dr. Cooper, who is indeed a 'sharp cookie', *had* recognized Gundar Coffee. Not from seeing him, but rather from prying out of Mr. Coffee's slim details a logical assessment of just who would negotiate such a commission.

"Blind hunch? How about that? ...No, it's not at my end. If it's not in your backyard then it must be somebody you met when you were playing Clifford Waxout."

Engrossing enough Mr. Coffee was correct, though neither of us recognized it at the time.

"So that's it, Mandrell. The sooner you give the folks Clifford Waxout's body to feed on the sooner we get all the FBI boys and the Secret Service guys put to bed."

"And you are serious you intend to withhold the fee until I have provided the body?"

"Not only provided it, Pal, but provided it someplace where the Secret Service can get their hands on it. Not FBI, not any hick-town police chief. The Service has taken a real black eye on this thing and I've got friends over there. They need help."

"Yes," I sighed as I slumped down in my seat. "Friends frequently do. But as long as one has business acquaintances whom one can cheat out of a legitimate fee, why then one can afford to be generous to friends."

"Where are we going?" Coffee asked. Our aircraft had slowed and you could feel our descent.

"To a small airport outside Leonardo, New Jersey. I have a car there. You may ride the aircraft back to Newark if you wish."

"Where are you going? Back into New York?"

"Where else can I go?" I raged at him. "I'm going for Clifford Waxout!"

"That's the spirit, old buddy," he laughed. "You bring in Cliff and I'll tap a little secret drawer in a national cash register for your fee."

"Fees, Mr. Coffee, fees. Plural. This Waxout business is a totally separate commission and will be negotiated as such. And believe me Mr. Waxout's remains shall not change hands until those fees are in my account. While I have a degree of knowledge regarding the indebtedness incurred by your government each year, and the economic factors that necessitates it, I have no intention of allocating my fee to alleviating any portion of that national debt. Did you think to solve your poverty problems with the meager funds stolen from my firm?"

"Don't worry, Mandrell, we'll work something out. But I don't see this Clifford Waxout thing—" He eased back in his seat, drawing his rather formidable negotiator's robes around him, around the national cash register, "as being as big a job as the Senator Dempsey thing, you know? So I don't see the second fee as being as big as the first, right?"

"We will indeed work something out," I said, my anger still in my voice. "Before we part on this day. And please be advised of one other item, Mr. Coffee. Please tell your employer that his personal idiosyncrasies are totally his own. I will not brook with his applying them to our agreement."

"Wadda you mean?"

"I will want my fee in a single lump sum, Mr. Coffee. Not in 76 separate installments."

AFTERWORD

My dad wrote this book in 1975 and sent it off to his publishers, Betty and Ian Ballantine. Even though it had been twelve years since the assassination of President John F. Kennedy, the mutual consensus was that the American people were not fully healed, were not ready to make light of the demise of an individual whom held possession of the highest office in the land. The manuscript was boxed up and closeted for thirty years.

Eventually the book titled, *Shoot the President, Are You Mad?* was brought to light and The Outfit agreed to publish it. My father passed on in 1986 but I believe he would be unabashedly delighted that yet another Mandrell commission was available to the public. My mother, who passed away this year, was thrilled at the prospect of this new publication. She was my father's biggest and most devoted fan.

I know my parents are toasting the release of this long forgotten Mandrell episode wherever they may be. I also know my six siblings and I are eternally grateful for the love, creativity and humor they gave us every day of our lives.

Liz (McAuliffe) Gollen
Idaho, 2009

CPSIA information can be obtained at www.ICGtesting.com
Printed in the USA
LVOW091401301111

257171LV00001B/162/P